PSYCHONAUTICA

PAUL DORU MUGUR

PSYCHONAUTICA

short stories

TRANSLATED FROM ROMANIAN BY

Sanda Ionescu and Christopher Sawyer-Lauçanno

First published in Romanian with the title "Psihonautica" by Curtea Veche Publishing House, Bucharest, 2009.

LIBRARY OF CONGRESS CATALOGING-IN-PUBLICATION DATA

Psychonautica
Authored by Paul Doru Mugur

ISBN: 9798985965919
LCCN: 2022943440

CONTENTS

zerlendi@shambhala.com

EDITORIAL NOTE:

In the winter of 1940, Mircea Eliade published "The Secret of Dr. Honigberger" in the Royal Foundations Magazine. The author admitted that in his text he wove elements of reality (Honigberger's actual historical existence, his own personal experiences in Rishikesh) and fiction so tightly together, that only "an informed reader could distinguish fact from imagination."

To summarise the story:

Eliade, a young Orientalist (the story is written in the first person), returns to Bucharest after a trip to India and is invited by an unknown lady to examine the collection of Oriental books and artifacts of her late husband, Dr. Zerlendi, who had disappeared more than twenty years before under mysterious circumstances.

While examining the materials that the doctor had amassed with the intention of writing a biography of Martin Honigberger, a 19th century surgeon and traveller of German descent, Eliade stumbles across a notebook in which Dr. Zerlendi kept a journal for two and a half years, written in Romanian but using the Sanskrit alphabet. Unwilling to interrupt his reading, Eliade takes the notebook home with him.

He is deeply impressed with the paranormal experiences recounted by Dr. Zerlendi, who had managed to attain invisibility while searching for the mythical kingdom of Shambhala, but was never able to regain his human form. Eliade tries on several occasions to return the notebook to the family and to share with them its contents, but without success.

Finally, he manages to meet Mrs. Zerlendi again, but she maintains—much to his surprise—that she has never met him before and that all her husband's books had been sold twenty years ago.

In conclusion, Eliade briefly notes that he does have a possible explanation for all of this, but he prefers, for some reason, to keep it a secret that he refuses to share. For half a century, until Eliade's death in 1987, hundreds of readers have tried to decipher the mystery of this strange tale. Eliade himself resisted any kind of pressure and insisted that that story was just fiction, nothing else.

Imagine our surprise then, when last week we received a message with "The Secret of Dr. Honigberger" in its subject line in our bulk mail folder, used mainly for marketing offers. At first, I thought that the author had sent us some comments for our new "Reading Notes" section in the Respiro journal, in response to our invitation issued across multiple discussion threads. But the message was full of errors. For example, the date seemed to be 10th of September, 2030, and the text appeared to be cut here and there. The email address was from "shambhala.com." After a Google search, I discovered this belonged to an independent publisher specializing in "books dedicated to mystical self-development." I tried to contact the author of the message several times, but to no avail. Every single time, that naughty little Yahoo mail devil, Mailer-Daemon, would solemnly announce that no such email address existed. One of our techie volunteers suggested that the address could be a restricted-access one, so we would need a special code to unlock it, or else the text could have been sent from some unknown server, creating a virus and changing the address and the content of a message destined for our *literary review. In any case, the author had to be an able hacker. Our techie guy reassured us that the possibility of having some sort of telepathy between the human brain and the Internet was impossible, technically speaking. Herr Doktor Horst Kurz, a respected scholar in German studies, kindly informed us that the German quote was from a poem by Rainer Maria Rilke, about music, written in Munich, the night of January 11th, 1918. When I looked back at the story "The Secret of Dr. Honigberger," I was astounded to discover that Dr. Zerlendi's diary stops exactly on the 10th of September, 1910. Below you will find the exact message, just as we received it.*

From: zerlendi@shambhala.com
To: revistarespiro@yahoo.com
Date: Fri, 10 September 2030, 9:15:59
Subject: The Secret of Dr. Honigberger

----------------interrupted message----------------

"As large as the external space, as vast as all the space that exists is the space inside the heart—for inside you will find everything inseparable, heaven and earth, fire and air, sun and moon, lightning and stars, whatever is here in the world, and whatever is not, whatever has been or will be, all is inseparable here."

The Mandala of our destiny rests beyond the horizon, in that hall where once a century all the sub-lunar forms gather and try to entice us with their never-ending dance.

He who can restrain himself from small talk in this hall, watching this performance that is beyond words, will achieve the deeper understanding that his bias to action comes from that unique vibratory point. His destiny will be to build up his sphere in an endless solitude. The illusion produced in all the other spheres, more or less narrow, will become clear to him, and he will be able to avoid it.

Thus, the sage will not lose his head when confronted by transient and rushed storytellers. Without remorse, he will cut off the soiled knots of the temptation of believing their lies.

----------------interrupted message----------------

First you have to choose a subject. In my case, I had decided to write my autobiography. No big deal, at first glance, but in my case the obstacles were almost insurmountable. The idea of writing about phenomena that seem so unreal compared to our normal existence is utterly fanciful. How can you write the history of a transparent cloud or of a summer morning? How can you hope to be understood when your entire being has become, as the poet says, "*Du Zeit, die senkrecht steht auf der Richtung vergehender Herzen?*" Fiction is the only alternative, with its lax restrictions and apparently pointless games.

That was the only way in which I could suggest to readers, as discreetly as does the scent of a subtle, evanescent perfume, that there is something deeper there, that beyond the thin veil of the fantasy tales, there is a terrible reality, an overwhelming presence.

It's clear now why I needed a professional, a fiction writer. But what kind of a writer? It was evident to me that I needed someone who was inspired, a visionary, a lunatic even, who had experimented somewhat with yoga and meditation techniques. How to find him? Where could I find this rare combination?

Even now, 90 years on, I smile when I remember Mircea. Mircea, not Eliade, not Mircea Eliade, the writer, philosopher, academic, historian of religions, etc., etc., etc., not the big name, just Mircea, the short-sighted adolescent, Mircea, the fearless, blameless knight who had set out to conquer the world of the spirit, Mircea, tireless Mircea. I was undoubtedly lucky to meet him.

OK, so now I had a subject and a writer, now for the trickiest part: communicating with your ghost writer.

Mircea was perfect not just because of his talent as a writer or his encyclopedic knowledge that went well beyond just Oriental Studies. Far more important than all of these was the intrinsic harmony between us. Our internal voices, *nostra verbum mentis*, were so alike that, at first, he had no doubts about what lay behind the impulse to write about the experiences of the mysterious Dr. Zerlendi, as he liked to call me.

I tried to infiltrate his dreams as discreetly as possible just before he awakened with the information I considered essential, so that he could remember it well. This gave him sufficient direction for his imagination to follow the route laid down by me, while leaving him enough room to feel that it was pure invention, the fruit of his inspiration.

Honigberger, of course, was a red herring. The passage that Mircea found so fascinating, the story of the fakir Haridas who was buried alive for 40 days by controlling his breath, was inserted by Honigberger in between descriptions of bloody battles for power at the Punjabi court, as was the equally strange story of another fakir who was immune to viper poison, because he was secretly ingesting homeopathic doses of arsenic.

These baroque stories, along with the exaggerated care with which Honigberger presents them, show us at once that the author wants to draw attention to himself, rather than tell credible stories.

Mircea, however, who had also been away from home in India for a long time, was charmed by Honigberger's sentimental style. The latter decided all of a sudden to leave the Punjab and return to Brașov: "In spite of my many lucrative businesses, I was homesick, for I had not been home in many years, so all thoughts and actions focused on the plan to return home. I was so obsessed with this idea that even if I had been offered the Koh-i-noor (estimated value: half a million) to stay there for the rest of my life, I would have categorically refused it."

I would just point out in passing Honigberger's materialism, his measuring his homesickness not against some spiritual achievement, but against a prosaic diamond, noting at once its monetary value so as to place some value on his nostalgia.

The main reason why I suggested Honigberger to him was that it was the way to reach Sándor, Korosi Csoma Sándor.

Honigberger and Csoma Körösi had left Transylvania to go east at roughly the same time. Honigberger's pilgrimage started in 1815 and never took him further than the Punjab. Csoma of Körösi

Sándor, however, who went to the Orient to discover the origins of the Hungarian language, spent nearly twenty years in Tibet and India, quite a bit of it together with the honorable Sang-gye Pun-tsong, a Tibetan monk of vast erudition, who had been tasked by the monarch in Ladakh with the mission to help Sándor in his philological quest.

Martin and Sándor never met, but the painter August Schoefft, who painted the only authentic portrait of Csoma of Körösi, was a very good friend of Honigberger's, and the latter wrote about him in his eclectic Asian travel journal. Then there was Dr. Gerard, to whom Martin gave his coin collection, who was also a good friend of Sándor's. And of course, General Allard, with whom Sándor had travelled in 1822 through Afghanistan, who also took a trunk full of antiquities to Martin in Bordeaux. The trunk also contained a Chintamani rug that Sándor had sent to Martin, asking him to take it back home. The rug, full of Shambhalic symbols, was later donated by Honigberger to the Black Church in Brașov, where it can be seen today, unless the moths have gotten to it.

Anyway, there were multiple links and Mircea knew them well. I told him so many times: Körösi Csoma Sándor, Körösi Csoma Sándor, Körösi Csoma Sándor... I even capitalised on his admiration for Jung's works by showing him a C-shaped key with SOMA written on it in huge letters and which hung on a silver chain on the stalk of a lotus with eight petals. Yet, in spite of all this, he refused to utter a word about Körösi Csoma Sándor. The explanation is simple, embarrassingly simple. Mircea noted somewhere that I was "passionate about the history of our people and the history of medicine." I'm almost sure that he was projecting his own obsessions onto me at this point. Looking at it from a distance, it all becomes clear. In the period between the two World Wars, Europe was a boiling cauldron of political, racial and nationalist problems. So how could a true-blue Romanian like Mircea, a patriotic and engaged intellectual, sit up and praise Sándor, Körösi Csoma Sándor, a Hungarian national hero, that the Japanese had declared to be a Bodhisattva back in 1933?

Mircea does not even mention Sándor in passing, but he does write that he "examined Honigberger's book for any details of occult practices that the good doctor appears to have been familiar with." And then he adds: "In reality, Honigberger had not only been to Kashmir, but also to Tibet, or he had at least studied occult pharmacology in one of the monasteries in the Himalaya, and this botanical research was just a pretext." Pretext? Honigberger didn't know a word of Tibetan, so the suggestion that he might have been initiated there in some esoteric science would make any close reader of his biography laugh derisively.

The reason for the intense correspondence between Sándor and Martin, which the latter had initiated and maintained throughout Sándor's stay in India, was an article that Sándor had published in 1835, in the prestigious *Journal of the Asian Society* in Bengal. The article, more than 20 pages long, proposed a detailed analysis of *rGyud-bshi*, a classic Tibetan medical document, made up of four chapters, that Sándor had studied together with the lama Sang-gye Pun-tsong, the same lama who was also the leading physician of the Ladakh royal court. In the fourth chapter, which the Tibetans believe was dictated at the dawn of history by Sangs-rGyas sMan-bla, the Buddha of medicine, there are indications on how to use several hundred medical herbs. Honigberger was very keen to learn more about these, and then he included them in his second volume of travel journals in the Orient, without any reference or acknowledgements. So that's where his advanced knowledge of occult pharmacology derives from!

----------------interrupted message----------

If he had at least mentioned his name, at least that, then some passionate reader would have continued searching. And would have discovered instantly, that in the story that I was trying to convey to Mircea, Honigberger was a mere secondary figure, a waiting room for Körösi Csoma Sándor.

Körösi Csoma Sándor was the first European to read the original texts referring to Shambhala, the word that he translates as "the source of eternal happiness," "the fabulous territory to the North, with the capital of Kalapa, splendid city, place of residence for many illustrious rulers of Shambhala, situated between 45 and 50 degrees northern latitude, beyond Sita and Jaxartes, where the days grow by 12 Indian hours between spring equinox and summer solstice, or 4 hours 48 minutes, according to the European system." This extract from an article that Körösi Csoma Sándor had published in 1833 in the 14th edition of the same Journal of the Asian Society was well-known to Mircea; he could have recited it at any time from memory.

Mircea had discovered, of course, that Csoma of Körösi's biography was the one that was full of mysteries, not the one of Martin Honigberger.

For instance, in December 1839, to everyone's great surprise, Körösi Csoma Sándor donates his entire collection of rare Tibetan manuscripts to the priest Malan, the secretary of the Asian Society, who was then in Calcutta, on his way back to England. Then there was that famous letter dated 9th February, 1842, written to Torrens, the new secretary of the Asian Society, in which Csoma of Körösi announces his decision to set off for the Himalayas and "tour around Central Asia."

No other European got closer to the essence of Shambhala than Csoma of Körösi, and Mircea knew it. There is such a massive gap between Csoma of Körösi, who compiled the first Tibetan-English dictionary and a grammar of the Tibetan language, both so thorough that they were still in use a century after their first publication in 1834, and Martin Honigberger, who could barely muster two or three words in Sanskrit.

My frustration and disappointment now appear ridiculous. How can a muse complain that the artist has betrayed her expectations?

Shambhala did hold an extraordinary fascination for Mircea: I only had to mention the name and the whole story became embedded with this mysterious kingdom.

Not even Mircea could escape dualism, that European disease that dates back to Aristotles. Even in regards to Shambhala, there was a war raging inside him. On the one hand, his rational mind was telling him that the place could only be found in a "qualitative space different from the profane one," and that you could only access it after "intense and laborious spiritual preparation." In other words, there is no geographic reality to this country. Yet, on the other hand, he continues to talk about that "green miracle between snow-capped mountains, those strange houses, ageless people who say so little yet understand each other's thoughts." He was blinded, as so many others were, by Nicholas Roerich's thumping rhetoric: "If it weren't for them, who think and pray for all the others, the entire continent would be shaken by demonic forces, which the modern world has unleashed since the Renaissance. Are we Europeans doomed? Is there nothing left to do for this world that is a victim to obscure spiritual forces that take it unknowingly to cataclysm? I am afraid that Europe will have the same fate as Atlantis and that all too soon it will sink into the water. If only people were aware that it is the spiritual forces from Shambhala that prevent this tragic change of axis of our globe, as geologists can tell you, which will tumble our world into water and give birth to some new continent."

This discourse would be pathetic, of course, if it were at least original. But Mircea, perhaps out of politeness, prefers just to copy the aberrations of the theosophists without even acknowledging them.

For me, however, Shambhala was merely the hook to help him remember the dream as clearly as possible.

----------------interrupted message----------------

Mircea did figure out at some point that inspiration only seemed to come to him when he was asleep. But that didn't upset him at all. On the contrary, he thought that was a good sign, that he could remember all of his dreams in such precise detail. He generously peppers the story with clues that show to the careful reader a dream-like origin. Shambhala, Smaranda, Sofia, S. Street, and of course Sándor, all starting with the same letter.

S is by no means the archetype of the winding road, full of temptations, the means of acquiring knowledge through wisdom, of the primeval snake, etc., etc., as someone with a passion for hermeneutics might suspect. No, it was simply the purple monogram on the pillow that he was sleeping on when I started interfering with his dreams.

"Anyway, what is reality other than a dream?" he started telling himself. Since this idea was so precious to Mircea—the ultimate truth for an artist to aspire to—that helped me immensely. Because he considered a priori that all that was happening to him in his dreams was merely an attempt for his innermost desires to find symbolic fulfilment, he did not suspect for a long time the reason behind the extraordinary coherence of his experiences in the realm of Morpheus. But at some point, he realised that his dreams were not his own. That passage in which he describes Sofia looking at me in her dream and getting frightened—that is, of course, drawn from his own experience. He suddenly felt my presence there, in the midst of his dream. He woke up and panicked.

At first, I thought that would be beneficial, as I believed that his anxiety could recreate that authenticity that the text had lost since Mircea stopped writing down the dreams through which I sought to communicate with him.

Unfortunately, he became worried that evil forces were possessing him, so he decided to give me up for good and avoid any explanation regarding the results of my quest. The end of the story, consequently, becomes a kind of exorcism, rather against my wishes. Well, that's as good a way to end a story as any, especially one of which not even the narrator can make any sense. Total confusion, which Mircea tried to mask (unsuccessfully, one might add) by hinting that he had some further explanations that he could not divulge without the agreement of all those concerned. What agreement could he possibly want, when we had ceased all forms of communication, and Shambhala remained somewhere far away, unattainable, within a dream by a dreamer unknown? That's the way it worked out! And all because of some silly superstitions he fell for...

It's taken me a whole century to get back in touch. Now the electronic brains are complex enough that I do not require any intermediaries. Interference. The law of resonance operates not only at the spatial level, but also at the temporal one. Interference. Between isomorphic structures information can be transmitted instantly, regardless...

----------------interrupted message----------------

At last, the world will know the name, the name of my guide, the name that Mircea obstinately avoided mentioning.

Every time I read "The Secret of Dr. Honigberger," I have a strange feeling. The words there are like a mirror in which, no matter from what angle I look, I cannot see myself. Sometimes I wonder if I am not myself some involuntary double, telling the story of a shadow that was never mine.

----------------interrupted message----------------

Then you will reach the final obstacle on your journey—a wall of mountains so high, so steep, that even eagles fear to cross it.

Goring the sky with their sharpness, the peaks soar above like giant demons blocking your way, destroying all hope. Do not be afraid: remember that the spirit can overcome any obstacle. Cast aside all your doubts and proceed. Let the clear light of understanding disperse your fears, and your illusions will dissolve like the night shadows at dawn. Remember that you can fly.

And then, below, you will see the cities of Shambhala, glittering among the snowy mountains like the stars in the Milky Way. Flowers of light to scatter the last vestiges of ignorance, and make you whole and happy once more, fresh at the journey's start, forgetting all the trials you have been through.

The Psychonaut

« il allait lentement, le plus lentement possible
pour que son ame pût éventuellement rattraper son corps. »
HENRI MICHAUX

Hey, you over there! You guys, you netheads, be careful,
guys, it's no joke! I know you think all these gadgets are cool,
this online chat, e-groups, animated gifs, and all that crap,
but watch out, you're playing with fire, bro! I know 'cause I
was just like you, chat-chat here, chat-chat there, combing my
hair on the webcam all day long. I know, I know the score
all right—the hottest MP3s, free film movie downloads, flash
animation—I tell you; I would have voted hand-on-mouse
for all of that!

But boys, I wholeheartedly advise you to give up all of
these tricks while there's time. The computer is like Aladdin's
lamp, if you rub it up the wrong way, the genie loses his temper
and bye-bye, Aladdin! So what's your name, little boy? How
now, brown cow…

Honestly, I'm not being funny. I've been playing around
with computers since I was a kid, my foundation years were
computer games' years. At sixteen I was such an established
hacker that the boys in the city hired me to oversee their computer virus programs. The wolf in sheep's clothing, eh? No, I'm
not giving you my CV now to show off or something, just to

prove that I'm not one of those guys who plugs the zip drive into the juice blender!

At eighteen I invested a little money into a company selling all sorts of stuff on the Internet and, a few months later, I was waving hello to Uncle Bill and Aunt Hillary from a mansion across the road, complete with swimming pool and nice English lawn. But of course, Sod's Law, easy come, easy go, the money went. I stuck the small change I had left into computer games—my passion—and a teensy studio-flat in Williamsburg. And of course, loads and loads of computer games. I wasn't that keen on sophisticated stuff like Warcraft, Black & White, or strategy games, no siree, I was too busy wandering around mazes and corridors collecting all sorts of objects and shooting down elves and monsters. I would munch on chips and bagels with lox, sipping ice tea and play on till the chair stuck to my butt.

It all started with the ceiling fan. I was lying on my bed, with a cigarette in my left hand, not thinking of anything in particular, just chilling out. The room was steaming like a jungle—if you've ever been dehydrated in the Nueva York in July, you'll know what I mean.

So, as I was saying, I was looking up with no particular intention or attention, when suddenly I see the fan blades slowing down, the five blades hiccupping to a halt, till they seemed mired in the muggy air like in sticky toffee.

"Power cut," I said to myself, but the light was still on, and there were some strange sounds coming from the street, a sort of growling. Just as suddenly, the fan started moving again, creating that circle on the ceiling.

A few days later, it happens again. This time, it lasts a little longer. I had time to go to the kitchen and switch on the fan there, which also moved slowly, like in a movie played in slow motion.

I didn't know what to make of it, until one afternoon, when my neighbor Virgil, a black guy from Jamaica, mad about jazz, came knocking at my door. Virgil gave me a broad smile and thrust a stack of dirty, tattered old records at me, probably gathered in haste from some garbage-tip, saying: "Come on, white boy, let's see what's going on with these vinyls."

I rummaged around the garage for about twenty minutes till I found the old record player that my ol' man used to listen to his Elvis singles on, then I struggled up the stairs with it. I picked up a record at random and put it on, taking care with the blunt needle. The room filled with the shrill sound of a trumpet. Virgil had gone, probably to search for some cold drinks in the fridge.

The music was cool, Gillespie in his glory days. Suddenly, Virgil appears with a look on his face as if his guts were turning to liquid. He covered his ears and yelled something. I couldn't hear a word he was saying, but his body language was pretty clear, so I stopped the music.

"What's with these yowling sounds, man? You idiot, you've put it on 78. Can't you see it's moving too fast, never had a turntable in your life?"

I didn't answer. What could I say? I changed the speed but the notes sounded dragged out and baggy, the song seemed to be a funeral march.

After Virgil left, I put all the records on 78 again, listening to them carefully. I was beginning to catch on. I then picked up my tape recorder and put on a Dylan tape on fast-forward. I could hear it perfectly clearly, no sweat. I switched on my VCR and put on *Breakfast at Tiffany's*, my favorite movie. I watched the whole thing in 4 minutes 37 seconds.

All of a sudden, goodness knows how, I had time. All my life I had wanted more time, not to have to rush from here to there like some mad ping-pong ball. And now, this gift had landed in my lap. I was delirious with joy. Hundreds of MP3 files I had never gotten around to listening to. All the movies I had put off watching. The shop assistant at Blockbusters stared at me like I was an alien when she saw me leaving with 30 video tapes in my arms.

And then there were the computer games. I could now go straight to the last level and fry their little monster brains right out of their heads!

I had some priorities. For instance, that impertinent Deep Blue. I had to put him back in his place ASAP.

I trained *illico-presto* online and, a few thousand rapid-fire games later, with a few international chess masters beaten, I called the guys from IBM and said that I wanted to play their machine. At first, they were having none of it, but after I showed them my Internet records, they agreed on a friendly game. I beat Ol' Mister Blue 19-0, and in that last game, he played so badly that I think a couple of his fuses blew up.

"Faster than light" screamed the headline on the front page of the *New York Times.* "Brooklyn youth beats Deep Blue without losing a game."

I was on a roll once more. Money started pouring in. I stayed in Williamsburg—for those of you who don't know Brooklyn, I'm tellin' ya, it's the only decent place to stay in this area—and moved into a loft in which you could have easily parked six of those stretch limos without even scratching their paintwork.

I'd become the flavor of the month overnight. My phone was blowing up, hundreds of emails poured into my Inbox from my fans, everyone in the whole wide world suddenly loved me and was concerned about my delicate health.

One evening I was in Tarantino's East-side bar, *Good Guy Eddie*, I was totally smashed, and the guy seemed cool. He told me his name was Larry Wachowsky and he loved making movies. He told me some things about *The Matrix*. The ideas seemed OK, so I told him about the speed thing. "Speed, man, speed is the key to the kingdom," I said. He thanked me enthusiastically, and, since Keanu Reeves and I are like two peas in a pod, I heard the film was quite a success. Just kidding! But what is interesting is that this is how people started hearing about psychonauts. But don't let me jump the gun here!

The downside of all of this was that I was beginning to lose my sense of smell and taste. My neural circuits had probably speeded up so much that they no longer registered information coming at them through the slower channels. I switched to spicy, spicier, spiciest food, until even the hottest chile peppers couldn't touch me. If you're not mad about Mexican food, Red Savina Habaneros ain't gonna mean much to you. But this crazy guy called Wilbur Scoville was so hooked on hot peppers, that he scored all of the hot chiles in this world. Sweet red peppers were zero, while the flamethrowers called Red Savina Habaneros can go up to half a million points, if fresh and well cooked. Multiply half a million units with a ton to imagine the amount of water needed to get rid of the burn. An earthquake of this magnitude would be like the Big Bang. Mexican and Indian chefs got to know me as a rare animal: "the crazy guy that eats fire for food." Sadly, I also got some hemorrhoids from that and couldn't sit down for a couple of weeks. As a result, I had to give up my combat sport with the peppers before I managed to establish some world record there.

But the boys from NASA have an answer for everything. I put in a special order and got to eat food for astronauts, which stimulates the sense of taste, while somehow bypassing the taste buds. I ain't got a clue how they do that, the prospectus for it is so tersely written that I wouldn't be surprised to hear it's some military secret. So now I was paying the equivalent of the monthly salary of a taxi-driver in Bahrain for my breakfast—and if you're a taxi-driver in Bahrain, you know for sure what I mean ;-)

I don't remember how I stumbled over the website. Psychonautica belongs to the kind of e-zones on the dark web that require a reaction speed well above those of your average web surfer. Whenever you try to access a psychonautic site, you invariably receive the message: 'Site not found.' Only a psychonaut can read the information available there in a fraction of a second. The hyperlinks disappear faster than you can blink. Psychonauts use the Web not only to support their underground network, but also as a fabulous source of income. Naturally, they want to keep a profile as low as possible.

They use the vast computational power of the Web to solve all sorts of complex issues that go way beyond the operational capacity of any ordinary computer. And for this, they get paid really well by all the corporations hungry to get solutions ahead of the competition—and they never ask awkward questions, of course. When an ordinary user chooses a URL (uniform resource locator) and asks for a webpage, the browser opens a TCP (transmission control protocol) and connects to a webserver. It then creates a HTPR (hypertext transmission protocol request) using that TCP connection. If the request is accepted, the message flows back in bits using the IP (internet protocol) via the same TCP and, finally, before reaching the browser, the message is rebuilt entirely anew.

Online, every act of communication presupposes some logical, mathematical operation. The trick is to use the dialogue between servers not to actually communicate anything, but to analyze data distributed amongst millions of computers, and to get them to work for you without realizing it.

Nope, the Web is by no means that democratic world praised to the heavens by cyber-geeks. This asymmetrical network contains some tens of thousands of key nodes that are super-connected, compared to their poor cousins, the ordinary servers. If these key nodes fail, you can wave goodbye to the Internet. Everyone's heard of the Ghost in the Machine, the New Electronic Messiah, that the psychonauts associate with Moore's law. But very few know that they use the superconnectivity of these ten thousand nodes to sponsor all their projects in anticipation of His Coming. Every time you connect to your favorite website, a little counter starts off an operation that slows your access down by a millisecond. *Time is money.* Your time in their pockets.

I've told you all this because I don't want you to think that psychonauts are a bunch of youngsters crazy about AI, working devotedly and selflessly to bring about Singularity, which is what they call the moment when electronic brain power will surpass the human mind. Sure, any story sounds good on film or between the covers of a book. Any utopia looks great at a distance and sounds fascinating as long as you're not involved in it. Have no illusions, the Net is a jungle which follows the rules of the jungle: eat or be eaten!

But let me get back to that site. The first page said roughly as follows: "Welcome to Psychonautica, the first site specializing in mind travel." Then a series of explanations followed:

"The first psychic speed is 10 to the power of 18 bytes per second, about ten times higher than the processing ability of a normal human brain. That's what got you onto this website. No big deal. A couple of doses of speed, a few good reflexes and here you are! But only if you manage to cross the barrier to the second psychic speed of 10 to the power of 19 bytes per second, that's when your journey begins in earnest. But drugs won't help you there. To start your initiation, you need to have a special calling. Reaching the second psychic speed is not for world record hunters or thrill seekers, it's only for those who are truly committed to exploring their inner world."

I set to work instantly. My mind was learning to move faster and faster. I could now effortlessly distinguish the batting of the wings of a fly, or hear every note in the most complex cacophony of sounds.

At first the training involved thinking without words. Once you get near the second psychic speed, thinking in words becomes an unintelligible jumble like IcanthinkcosIdontknowwheretoputthecomma.

I'd ordered five flat screen monitors, round like portholes. I'd soundproofed all the windows so no noise could penetrate from outside. All my walls were doubly insulated, while heavy black velvet curtains kept out the light. I had created all the conditions to progress unhindered.

In the blackness of my study, the five monitors shone like blue ice, casting a mysterious, cold light around the room. Like an Eskimo I sat there fishing for information. You have to fall for it, man.

Maybe you've had this experience: you've had a dream that seemed to last for hours, even if it only took a few minutes. The principle upon which psychonautics operates is to induce a dream-like state by bombarding the retina very rapidly with images. Kind of like a hyper-speed REM. In contrast to dreaming, however, you are perfectly lucid and capable of following each lightning flash of images, while your thoughts are guided towards the past or the future at phenomenal speed, such as you'd never get through normal memory or imagination.

Some images were vaguely familiar. I saw a young version of my mom wearing a brown check mini-skirt, smiling with her Cindy Crawford mole, trying to convince me to go to nursery school. It was morning, we were both in the kitchen, there were crumbs on the faded oilcloth on the table, I had just eaten a croissant. I moaned that the nursery was full of germs and wasn't she sorry to leave her child among strangers. Mom was laughing and saying I was showing signs of being a real heartbreaker already. Then I saw my dad in my grandparents' yard, repairing the chain on a blue bike with peeling paint. It was hot outside, the sun was shining through the foliage of the cherry tree, my dad was wearing shorts, squatting in front of the bike, his back shining with perspiration. Then I saw granddad, young, a salesman at Mr. Weissman's watch shop. With calm gestures, granddad was packing a pocket watch and chain into a small box lined with red satin.

The images were not necessarily chronological. Access was instant. There was no sense of time in this ancestral memory, everything was suspended, like some huge immobile simultaneity, from birth until the end of the world. But some images kept resurfacing, like lighthouses above the frozen ocean of information.

A woman riding a ginger-colored donkey
A man kneeling in front of a clump of earth
Three women washing their laundry in the river, singing
A girl with shaved hair eating snow
An old man under a tree in the rain
A mustachioed man emphatically kissing a woman, whose shoulders are quivering slightly

A young man arching his bow, closing his left eye
An old woman, with blue eyes, kneading dough
A little boy chasing after a dragonfly
A girl running through a pine forest
Two women drawing water from the well
A youth lying on the grass, watching the clouds
A little girl milking a goat

I saw a million such images. After a while, the people all started to have dark skins, then, gradually, they turned into some humanoid species with hairy faces, uttering some throaty sounds. Then this species was replaced by a mammal looking more like a weasel than a monkey. I then saw the horse species that I had learnt by heart when our teacher took us to the Natural History Museum: Merychippus, Mesohippus, Eohippus, then a period followed in which I seemed to be on the set of *Jurassic Park*, with all those noisy and dirty brontosauruses. Then the giant ferns of the Permian period, then the buzzy insects of Devonian, finally the blind fish of Cambrian. The first life forms were ovoid bacteria, nothing special at all. Then the images got more and more violent. Flashes of lightning, sparks, explosions, countless wreaths of light, billions of red-orange-yellow images. The last distinct image I had was of a single white pulsating point. Then suddenly all the images melted into a super-complex shape. In that split second, I could see all of time, all of space, all of the multidimensional mandalas of the world. Our universe was merely a leaf in the vast forest of universes. The leaf will grow, wither and die. And its place will be taken by another leaf that will have the same fate, and so on, leaves growing and dying, until the tree from which our universe sprung will wither and die too. But not the forest. The forest is eternal.

Look, you don't have to believe anything I tell you. Every journey I took, I found out more and more about the past and the future of this pluriverse, absolutely everything that is engraved there: the stars, the skies, the Earths floating around there. I won't tell you anything about the immediate future, because any of that sort of information would irrevocably change the configuration of the universe we're in. Let's put it like this: I like the next few episodes and I ain't gonna play Nostradamnus.

Yes, I've found out everything, everything my mind could take in. I had exhausted all the images on the website. But I still had no answer. The last page said:

"Congratulations. You've now attained the second psychic speed. You got very close to the third psychic speed, but unfortunately, we don't know what lies beyond. From now on, you're on your own. No one who has passed this threshold has ever come back to tell the tale."

Well, that wasn't too encouraging. My last few journeys changed me. For the worse. For example, any attempt to speak would end in inane mumbling. I'd never gone out much, but now I was incapable of speech. I stayed in all the time, ordering everything via the Internet. To answer the phone, I had ordered a voice synthesizer capable of translating my written messages into a metallic, emotionless voice. I didn't want to give up just yet. I could feel the solution was really close. I remembered a movie from the 1980s: some nutty professor experimenting with all sorts of hallucinogenic drugs while immersed in a tank filled with liquid. I had heard from the psychonauts that experimenting with drugs was useless, but the added bonus of reducing your sensorial impressions even further by immersion in a liquid—that sounded pretty cool.

I had enough space. I pretended I wanted to open an industrial-sized launderette, and got myself a huge washing machine, so big I could fit in it standing. I added a thermostat, so the water temperature would remain constant, close to body temperature. I changed its programming, so it wouldn't spin me whenever and wherever. Since I couldn't access the monitors directly and I was shielded from my Wifi, I connected my old games' helmet directly to a portable hard disk on which I downloaded some vectorial animation from a website.

I was eager to get started. Finally, I would find out what was behind this ridiculous game of hide-and-seek. I put on my helmet and special waterproof one-piece, and got into the machine. I had attached a Plexiglass bell on top of my helmet, and connected it to an oxygen bottle, which would keep me going for three hours. I looked rather cool. I think Laika would have barked enviously if she had seen me.

I don't remember anything about that journey other than the image of a giant sphere covered in tubes, like the gray cocoon of a silkworm. Then I lost it.

When I came to, I was in an empty white room, tied to a bed. Three years. It's taken me three years to regain my life. Because of the gigantic power consumption of my washing machine, I had blown all the fuses in the building. Total blackout. Fortunately, the landlord had the keys to my apartment. He found me shaking like an epileptic, eyes rolling, teeth chattering, and he dialed 911 immediately. After a few days in intensive care, I began to recover and they put me into a secure ward. The guys found it kind of hard to diagnose me: seizures of the temporal lobe, manic episodes, paranoid schizophrenia. Everyone had their own theory. What did it matter? Three years of purgatory. My mind is now like the engine of a second-hand Buick whose previous owner couldn't keep off the gas pedal... Still running though.

I started this tale, only half-jokingly, to warn you guys. Let go of your computer, let go of your games, forget the speed, the fast-forward culture and all that crap. I tell you: I've been there. All the way to the end. But it's a road that doesn't lead anywhere. Psychonautics is a dead-end road.

You know, my dears, I think I'm a lucky guy. Because in the end, I succeeded. I did it, man, and I am doing it right now. *I am looking her in the eyes.* And happiness floods into my soul faster than the third psychic speed.

Home Alone 5.0

A mobile phone lost in the sea
Is ringing and singing but never for me
ZUIHITSU

"What are you doing?"

"I'm reading. Who's this?"

"It doesn't matter. Tell, what are you reading?"

"What do you mean, it doesn't matter? It matters a lot to me! Do you expect me to tell you what I am reading when I don't even know who I'm talking to?"

"What use is it to know my name, my place of residence, my food preferences and other such minor details? Don't you think it's more important that someone is interested in what you are reading?"

"Why do you care what I am reading?"

"Are you ashamed of your reading matter? Anyway, you can tell me what you like, there's no way of checking."

"And why would I make confessions to a woman I have never met in my life?"

"Don't get angry, don't you realize it's much more interesting not to know to whom you are speaking. I could be anyone, and, instead of that exciting you and stimulating your imagination, you get annoyed. You'll never have to meet me. I promise that right now. I dialled this number entirely by

29

accident, I haven't got a clue what number I dialled. It's a ten-digit number and the chance of dialling it again is minute."

"Why are you doing this?"

"Look, see, I managed to spark your interest in the end. Now you want to find things out about me."

"Well, since you called anyway... I hope you did this to have a conversation, not a monologue. I am sure that you rang because you are lonely and bored and you needed a bit of a distraction. Come, admit that this is the reason, you didn't dial a random number to talk with someone, but to find someone disposed to listen to you. Tell me, you're a lone woman who is bored and calls unknown people, aren't you?"

"If it makes you feel better, let's say that's true. Now will you tell me what book you are reading?"

"I wasn't reading a book. I was reading the papers."

"What newspaper?"

"One of the dailies from here in town."

"What town is that?"

"You don't know what town you called?"

"No, didn't I tell you that I dialled the ten digits randomly. I must have dialled your town's prefix without even noticing. There, don't you feel better now that you realize I don't even know what town you're in? Tell me, do you read the papers daily?"

"Yes."

"Why?"

"To keep myself informed."

"And why do you feel the need to keep yourself informed? What are you looking for? What are you trying to find out? Why don't you go fishing? Why don't you go and watch a movie or go for a walk in the park? Why don't you watch TV? Why are you reading the paper of all things?"

"That's the first time anyone has asked me that. It's one of my habits. I come home from work, buy the newspaper at the smoke-shop around the corner, get home, eat something, make myself a cup of tea, sometimes I pour myself a little cherry liqueur, then I sit down comfortably in my armchair and read the paper. It relaxes me, gives me pleasure."

"Have you ever stopped to consider that you are a coward, that you are afraid to live, that you are swallowing other people's ideas without even chewing them? Does that relax you? Of course, it does, it takes minimal effort to read. Paper doesn't attack you, words don't besiege you. So you say you are comfortable? Do you know how comfortable it is to be outside, with no place to sleep, when it's cold and raining buckets down rain in buckets? People being born and dying, governments forming and disappearing, presidents getting assassinated, railway accidents, rapes, bestsellers you're never going to read—are these really the things that you're interested in, really? Tell me honestly, is this what you want to find, haven't you got anything better to do with your time?"

"Geez, that's all I needed, a frustrated intellectual and a psychoanalytic session over the phone! Why are you insulting me, Miss or maybe Madam, whatever? I thought we had established that you were calling because you were lonely, bored and needed a friendly chat. So tell me, what do you want from me, why are you saying all these things, why are you attacking me, you want me to get annoyed and bang down the receiver, is that it?"

"I'm sorry, I didn't mean to insult you, please forgive me. But seriously, don't you realize you are growing prematurely old? Don't you realize that you are actually reading the paper because of fear and, at the same time, in the secret hope that some day you are going to read your own obituary there?"

"So what concern is it of yours that I am growing old? That's my right, it's my freedom to live as I want and to die how I want. Whatever we do, we'll all grow old in the end. Since we started this chat on the phone, you yourself have grown older by a few minutes. That's life, what should I do, shall I commit suicide because I'm getting old? Do you think I've got nothing better to do than throw myself out the window because I know that I'm going to die some day anyway? Fat chance!"

"Please don't mention that word, please don't talk to me about suicide!"

"Why shouldn't I talk about suicide? Are you by any chance some weirdo that wants to commit suicide, and instead of reading my paper in peace, I'm wasting my time talking about all sorts of nonsense with a coward who can't quite bring herself to do it, so she picks up the receiver and dials some random number? You want to teach me about life? You call me a coward because I let others think for me, you of all people, the pot calling the kettle black? Who gives you the right to judge? Don't you realize you are the coward here? Yeah, sure, I understand, you don't want me to utter the word. Madam is sensitive. Open your eyes and look around. Why do you want to kill yourself? Have you reached the end of your rope? Can't bear things anymore? No strength to keep on going? No will to live? Oh, if only it were that simple! You don't like things anymore and bye-bye, life! If only you knew how many believed this before you, how many have been tempted to end this comedy once and for all. Talk about swallowing things without chewing, have you ever seriously thought about why you want to commit suicide?"

"You're talking about something you don't understand. Suicide has nothing to do with philosophy, logical arguments and sterile discussions. So what if I'm not original? I just have this unbearable pain and I want to end it. I'm desperate. I can't bear it anymore. Do you understand?"

"What do you expect from me, that I'll let you cry on my shoulder and play the comforter? What would you like me to say? That life is wonderful? That there are still so many things worth living for? That I should convince you to live, because there is always an unexpected solution just around the corner? Talk to you all night long until the morning light diminishes your depression? Keep you talking until you are too tired and powerless to do it? What strategy shall I use, how should I lie to you? Don't you realize that you are playing a petty game here? Don't you realize that I'd be telling you all of this just so that I can sleep contentedly afterwards? Why do I care about you? Who are you? Just an unknown woman who disturbs me and tries to find courage to either live or die by talking to an unknown man. Maybe I am a suicidal person too, who lacks the courage to do it. Maybe I too am at the end of my tether, maybe I too am desperate, and when you reminded me that I was growing old, that I have grown old, that I will continue growing old, slowly, invariably… maybe I will say to myself: OK, that's it! And throw myself from the roof. You called me hoping I could help you, but look now, without even meaning to, your death wish has contaminated me as well. Do you realize what a huge responsibility you took on by phoning someone randomly? Who am I? Have you got a clue who I am? Tell me, aren't you sorry you called now?"

"Sir, sir, stop, please stop, please, please stop harming yourself. I can see you are a very lonely person. You love to hear yourself speak, and you know now that all of these are constructs. You know just as well as I do that you would say anything now to stop me doing it. I know you are not as insensitive as you want to seem. You're posing, since no one could be that lacking in sensitivity. I know you care about me really. You can't not care. Tell me, would you like to meet me and get to know me better?"

"We started off on a first-name basis and now you are calling me 'sir'? You may have forgotten, but five minutes ago you promised we would never meet. What, now that you've met someone crazier than you, you've lost your will to commit suicide?"

"No, but I've grown to like you. I can confess now, I wasn't planning to commit suicide, not for a second. I just put on a bit of a show, because I thought that would be a good way to find out with whom I was dealing. I liked your voice from the outset and I thought I'd test you by pretending I wanted to commit suicide, and see how you'd react. Honestly, it's the first time I've done this."

"Well, and are you pleased now? Have I passed the test?"

"Yes, but that's not important now. Would you like my number?"

"No... Not yet."

"So... So I have to think that..."

''Yeah, you have to think that you were right. I am tired, I feel exhausted, old, I'm not in the mood for nonsense discussions at this time. To be honest, I am so fed up with all of this, with your silly games, in fact, I hate the phone, I hate speaking on the phone."

"Well, I hope you're not going to do something crazy now. I hope you're joking. I hope I haven't angered you so much that..."

"What do you want? Want me to say that I put on a show as well? To promise that I won't top myself after you hang up? What a grotesque game! What are we doing, playing Russian roulette over the phone? Bingo! Whose turn is it now to commit suicide? Anyway, what do you care, you've had your fun, maybe it even got you a bit excited. That's what you wanted, isn't it? A little escape from the everyday boredom. Well, I hope you will toss and turn all night now and maybe next time you will think twice before dialling a random number. And this trick, with the test, that's a cheap shot, believe me!"

"Sir, please…"

"That's enough, go to sleep now."

"But, sir…"

"Good night."

—

"Hello, yes?"

"Professor, sorry to disturb you, sir. My name's Robert and I'm a student of yours in the Bionics and Artificial Intelligence course. Together with Paul—I'm sure you remember Paul, because he always asks lots of questions at the end of each lecture—we created a simulator of telephone conversations between two complete strangers. Home Alone 5.0 is the name of the software. We thought we would try it out first on you, the specialist in Turing tests."

"We're really sorry if we wrecked your evening, we didn't do it deliberately. The program still needs a bit of work, and it was madness to start running tests so early, but we were bored, had drunk a couple of beers and thought, "Let's see what happens!" So we dialled your number and started it up. Please don't hold it against us! Our program is full of errors, and when we realized what direction the conversation was taking, we raised our arms in horror! Well, Paul and I are now in a horrible situation—don't be angry—but your reaction was rather surprising. We couldn't decide if you suspected something or if it was pure coincidence that you ended the conversation so abruptly. Please tell us if you realized, once you had hung up, that you were speaking to a computer?"

"Dear Robert, I'm sorry, but the professor is not at home."

"Well, who are you?"

"My name is George. I'm the automated answering machine. If you wish, you can leave a message after the beep."

The Pessoa Syndrome

for Kimba

I shut down my Inbox. Today was our boss's birthday, and the secretaries had filled the office with helium balloons in all the colors of the rainbow. It's well past six on Good Friday. We've had the speech, the congratulations, the singing 'Happy birthday to you' and all the required kissing. The boss had hung around with us for a while, then left, and we brought out the champagne and whisky and started chasing the balloons with colored thumbtacks. We were all kind of out of it after a short while. Someone found a hip-hop station and the little interns were waggling their heads like geese to the bass rhythm. The brokers were playing Blind Man's Bluff among the desks, bumping into photocopiers and coffee machines. Our office is partitioned off into several dozen cubicles, with white plastic dividers. They're about the size of the disabled toilets at Barnes and Noble.

I'm a quant. I've been working at this company since last spring. Investments, insurance, financial planning. You must know by heart now our ad, interrupting the Saturday night movie at the most exciting moments: "In a quicksand world, we are your rock. Lean on us, the whole world does: Atlas Investments."

Quant comes from quantitative analysis. A couple of times per month I get some folders full of data provided by the company's statisticians. I do some calculations, try to develop a model taking into account all the risk factors. I try to estimate the market fluctuations and the gains of potential investors. With a little bit of luck, a week or two later, I manage to convince the brokers how things stand and wipe the bewilderment off their faces. My conversations with them make me feel like a taxidermist trying to market crocodiles under the name of "bunny rabbits."

"I don't get it. This model is a fantasy. I don't see how it's going to work."

"Look closer. Can't you see the floppy ears now?"

"Ears? These are most definitely horns!"

"No way are they horns. Horns are rigid. I'll run a simulation for you, if you like, to show you how flexible these are."

"OK, OK, but why does it have six legs and two heads?"

"It's an updated version. These additions will make it more resilient to market forces."

"But isn't the tail too long?"

"Well, that's the whole point. If the market crashes, the investor minimizes his losses. The tail allows him to fall on his feet, like a cat."

"But I thought you said it was a bunny rabbit!"

All day long these brokers pester me with stupid questions, and the phone keeps ringing like in a betting shop, while I try to juggle equations. One comma to the left or right and I'm toast. I have to check the results hundreds of times to make sure I haven't made a mistake. This obsessive compulsion is essential to the quant's survival kit.

There are five more guys working as quants here in our firm. Special prizes at international competitions, maths or physics graduates, Ph.D.s, post-docs, tons of articles published in academic journals, all that crap. Our story, retold countless times by the *Wall Street Journal* and in the business section of the *New York Times*, is as dull as ditchwater.

It's nine o'clock, the alcohol has run out, so the party has moved to the Irish pub in SoHo. Cigarette smoke and the hot air of the brokers make for noxious fumes, so, under the pretext of an urgent deadline, I wish them a nice evening and head back to my office.

Lately it's been pouring down with projects, after all the fuss with the turn of the millennium. Since Maria left me three months ago, it isn't like I have anyone at home waiting for me. I prefer to work a bit longer rather than return to my place and watch paint dry.

At midnight I shut down Mathlab and logged onto the Internet. I checked my emails. I have to delete junk mail daily from my Inbox.

"Are you happy with the size of your penis? Click here and you will gain 2-3 inches, FOR SURE! Our penis-enlargement pro-gramme has the most competitive prices and your request will be treated in the utmost confidence. You will make your partner explode with pleasure."

"A night with me will change your life. Come on, dare to do it! I'm hot and humid. Waiting for you."

I entered a chat room, and then several others, but the dis-cussions were all about sex, sex, sex. At that time of night, the Internet seems to be full of strokers, one hand on the mouse, one hand… At least cavemen used to rub it to get some fire. Globalization, technology, all those silly slogans. A whole planet ready to ejaculate in unison. What should I do? Should I stay or should I go? Go where at this time of night? I was stuck between two chessboards. The outside one had yellow cabs rushing up and down it to the howl of ambulances and police sirens. The internal one, on the computer, had frustration pulsating on it at the speed of my modem's connection. I tossed a coin. The Internet won, so I thought I would educate myself a bit. I went onto Napster and downloaded some Miles Davis MP3s, then I went onto e-Bay. Books were listed third, after art and antiques. On the fiction page, the book covers were displayed one beneath the other. If you clicked on them, you could read a short description of the contents.

I was drawn toward a cover showing a man in a suit, tie and hat sitting at a table in front of an open window, through which you could see the ocean and a sailing boat. The man was reading. There must have been a mirror behind him, because you could see his back as well. The book was a collection of short stories by a guy called Pessoa. The review stated that the guy was an eccentric who had created 80 or so alter egos, each with their own name, profession and personal habits. Pessoa had invented a different style to fit in with the idiosyncrasies of each of his characters. Ricardo Reis, for example, was an epicurean, a doctor who wrote odes inspired by Horace. Alvaro de Campos was a naval engineer and passionate admirer of Walt Whitman. Alberto Caeiro was a simple shepherd, but the other two considered him their master in the art of living and writing. Fernando Pessoa, the man with 80 or more masks. A simple and effective idea. Columbus's egg.

Maybe this was the whole point of the Internet. Maybe, like the boy in "The Prince and the Pauper," we have been using the state seal to crack nuts. Have you ever thought that the Internet could be the embryo of an emerging mind? What if it's your own mind, or at least the multiple routines and subroutines of which it is made? To hell with chat rooms and stupid discussions! Communicating with others isn't the point. You are the point! Through the Internet you can find out things about yourself that no psychoanalyst, no matter how experienced, can drag out of you. It's only with yourself that you can be that candid. The Internet is the ideal catalyst, the perfect venue for the fancy dress ball. Check it out for yourself if you don't believe me. All you need is a computer and a high-speed connection, so you don't get bored waiting for the answers to the messages you are sending to yourself. I set up an e-forum in five minutes. It didn't take much longer to create and register a dozen email addresses on the Pessoa e-group. The night was still young. I didn't know then but that night would last for five and a half months.

LATIN_LOVER: I'm the pterodactyl inside you, that scaly creature with leathery wings that swallowed your ancestors 75 million years ago.

PAVLOV'S_DOG: Did it taste OK? You didn't get indigestion, did you?

BACKGROUND_NOISE: It's a fine day, a fine week, a fine month, a fine year. I bite a chunk of juicy happiness every minute of every day.

COCKADOODLEDOO: Cockadoodledoo!

GOURMANDE: Rose petal jam—you can spot the taste of it in absolutely everything…

CLICKONIT: Do you remember when you caught your hand in Lise's car door? I'm that black nail on your right thumb, you can't have forgotten?

SYMPATICO: The first rule of diplomacy: never tell your conversation partner anything that they might not like.

MNEMOTECHNICS: We have put everything in order: a before b, b before c, a before c, how can we remember how to order things? How come it doesn't all turn into a jumble in our heads? What we are now, what we've been... But what are we, what have we been? Merely the things we can remember... We are those things that we remember being... Take a pack of cards, mix them all up... *Les jeux sont faits... Rien ne va plus...* Then, suddenly, there's another one. Alter Iago?

ALTER IAGO: He was thinking so intensely about himself, that his face was covered with his self-image like a horror film being projected onto a screen.

BACKGROUND_NOISE: It's a fine day, a fine week, a fine month, a fine year. I bite a chunk of juicy happiness every minute of every day.

FLY_IN_A_JAR: Can you understand with the same intensity you reach when your retina is being pierced with red-hot needles that this is pure intellectual masturbation?

SYMPATICO: The second rule of diplomacy: if someone asks you a question you don't want to answer, say: why are you asking me this?

DADA: Explosions, lightning, scintillation, blink and unblink, nudging, starting, boiling and erupting, touching, merging,
sundering, illuminating, jumping, groping, rolling,
dismember, disentangle, distend,
dismantle, discern,
clarify, classify, specify, remorse.

MONTAGNERUSSE: Words, like numbers, have different degrees of elasticity. For instance, the word 'shunting track' is rough and ready like a 'four' in freshly poured concrete, while 'owl' is soft and cuddly like the number *pi*.

BACKGROUND_NOISE: It's a fine day, a fine week, a fine month, a fine year. I bite a chunk of juicy happiness every minute of every day.

121: Men's eyes, women's eyes, flirtatious eyes, seductive eyes, eyes to the floor, eyes to the sky, eyes staring straight at you but not seeing, eyes seeing you but not looking at you, imploring eyes, commanding eyes, weighing-you-up eyes, disdainful eyes, approving eyes, honey-colored eyes, sea-colored eyes, pine-colored eyes, eyes the color of dried tobacco leaves, steely eyes, wooden eyes.

GOURMANDE: Anchovy, you can spot the taste of anchovy in anything.

BABY: Gaga, gaga, yuck, mummy, oh mummy, mamaaaa!

121: Eyes like two dolphins, eyes in which you can lose yourself, eyes to stonewall you, unblinking eyes on a statue, darting eyes of a weasel, pedantic eyes, bellicose eyes, eyes that have seen nothing else but plains, eyes with long, curled eyelashes, eyes without eyelashes, eyes slanting up, eyes slanting down, eyes round like a bird's, eyes that have never seen a thing, eyes wide open, squinting eyes, a child's eyes, severe eyes, obedient eyes, indignant eyes, sincere eyes, eyes, thousands of eyes, thousands of glimpses.

JELLO: All eyelids are the same.

LATIN_LOVER: To be drunk on love, to dream of eyes, ankles, voices; to toss and turn in bed trembling with the desire to be with her, to have her there with you… how ridiculous, what a fool's game, what an obscenity, rolling your eyes like the metal balls in a Pachinko game… so many sighs, so much planning and scheming, and for what? For whom? To kiss her? To caress her? To enter her? To fill her up with your bodily fluids? To bite her, whip her, kill her, let her kill you, let yourself be cut into morsels, burnt alive, quartered… all for what, for whom? What horror, such an endless nightmare, is that what being alive is all about? I have a hard-on, therefore I am?

COCKADOODLEDOO: Cockadoodledoo!

MNEMOTECHNICS: Time is for people the obscure desire to reach that state of equilibrium that only the universe has.

PAVLOV'S_DOG: Noooo? Is that so? So that's why I can never remember where I put my glasses?

BACKGROUND_NOISE: It's a fine day, a fine week, a fine month, a fine year. I bite a chunk of juicy happiness every minute of every day.

ALTER_IAGO: In the morning, getting out of bed, shuffling unsteadily to the bathroom, hazy glance in the mirror, feel my bones cracking, a new beard, a new day, who am I? What if I were to wake up a different person every day? Again, and again, and again? Who am I, who are you? How do I know that I am not a different person? That I haven't been replaced secretly in my sleep? How do I know that you and I stay the same? I open my mouth as wide as I can and look in the mirror above the basin, I move real close, till the mirror fogs up. Through the fog, I can see my tongue, like an animal in a toothy cage— somewhere beyond that, I can spot a delicate, trembling little morsel of flesh: the uvula. I've always harboured a secret fascination with this gateway to my insides. I can imagine saliva sliding down the pharynx, then entering the drainpipe of the esophagus, passing through an opening shaped like a meat-eating plant and then, splash! landing with a thump in the acid bath of the stomach. Shake it to the left, shake it to the right, shake it all around, and the liquid then drains into the intestine, gushing down them like on a waterslide. The further it goes, the smellier it gets, until, yuckety-yuck, poo-ey, it reaches the sticky darkness of the rectum.

BABY: Poo, boo, moo!

ALTER_IAGO: Each one for ourselves, in those goddam tunnels, from the moment of birth, from the moment we descend through that narrow tunnel in a woman's pelvis, we just keep on falling, freefalling in a tunnel that is now so wide we no longer see its walls, except sometimes when we wake up all sweaty and tired from our nightmares. Then, at the very end, for a split second, the tunnel becomes clearly visible again, just for a tiny second we see that final tunnel, that freefall, just a second and that's it...

MONTAGNERUSSE: Any calculation is a matter of balance. All equations can be solved in the inner ear. The "equals" sign forms the beam of the balance scale, while the constants are the weights we add to the weighing pan.

LADYD: Death haven, death shore, death where no sound can reach you, no color touch you, death the dark realm, so calm, so serene... Death like the climax you feel approaching, so you start to moan and writhe, biting your lips till you draw blood, white death, endless night of death, arrested breath, death.

PAVLOV'S_DOG: Listen, lady, you gone off the rails or something, you dolling yourself up or what?

JELLO: Whaddya expect from a dumb blonde?

SYMPATICO: The third rule of diplomacy: never turn down compliments.

FLY_IN_A_JAR: You hang onto the thought that there must be a way out, like a drunk hanging onto his shadow.

BACKGROUND_NOISE: It's a fine day, a fine week, a fine month, a fine year. I bite a chunk of juicy happiness every minute of every day.

CLICKONIT: Coo, coo, mrdat, this morning I saw two pigeons making love—coo! The female pigeon was squatting, not making a sound. The male was all puffed up above her. Then the female tried to nibble him and, after a minute or so of fierce posturing, he flew away elsewhere.

MONTAGNERUSSE: Vertigo… rolling… spinning… lunging… pirouetting…one two three… which one's left, which one's right?

PAVLOV'S_DOG: You crazed fool, left hand cuts the cards, right hand gets the cards, simple.

LEFTEAR: I would fall in love with voices I'd heard only once over the phone, so I would phone people randomly, simply to discover new voices. I'd find all sorts of excuses to keep the owner of that voice talking, to keep on uttering the silliest little things, just so that I could continue bathing in the sound of their syllables, just so that their vowels would continue smashing against the consonants like waves on hidden rocks, whirling in unexpected currents, spurting up playfully or falling in a dizzying cascade. With the passion of a collector, I set out to find and listen to the most bizarre and unusual voices possible, dead actors' voices from film archives, dictators of yesteryear, market stall holders and ice-cream sellers, sports commentators, priests, new-born babes.

CLICKONIT: Finally clicked as to why I find the semicolon so disgusting. This morning I saw a greenish-brown, semi-colon shaped piece of dog poo, the masterpiece of a dog and its rushed owner, who risked a hundred dollar fine: please curb your dog!

MNEMOTECHNICS: And thus we should think about this transient world: a morning star, a whirlpool in a stream, a summer lightning, a flickering lamp, a ghost, a dream.

LEFTEAR: The waxen voices of the dying, the voices on loud-speakers at railway stations, the smacking sound of Indian voices, the tinkling sound of Chinese voices, the throaty sound of Arabic voices, the harsh sound of German voices, the commanding sound of Japanese voices, and the icy sound of Inuit voices—I was sometimes moved to tears by voices that I couldn't understand at all, because I thought I could detect a certain nostalgia for expressing things that cannot be expressed in words at all. Those voices were alive, trembling, vibrating, pulsating to their very own rhythm. When listening to those voices I sometimes thought I could distinguish the ventriloquist soul of the world itself, the sound-equivalent essence of life.

DADA: Desire, inventions, deceptions, labyrinths, exhaust-pipes,
    howling, mirrors, murmurs, nights, tossing,
        sunrise and sunset, lullabies,
            excuses, postponements, interjections,
                blunders, requests, madcap climbs,
siege

                and renouncement.

ONIRIKON: Numbers, numbers, numbers. Some people dream in color, in images, in adventures—I have only ever dreamt in numbers, numbers, numbers. And these numbers have given me everything that numbers can possibly give you: a carefree life, a life as light and pure as a snowflake.

MONTAGNERUSSE: Blinded, deafened, tasteless, odour-less, anesthetized, the only witness to my lack of feeling is the vertigo.

GOURMANDE: Pickled green tomatoes, you can spot the taste of them in absolutely everything.

LATIN_LOVER: The nudist beach, women lying in the sun, my fascination with the red thread peeking out of the hairy cunt. Laura with her rough tongue, I almost fell right over when she thrust it into my mouth. Georgeta's red lips, my first porn mag, the blue eagle tattoo right under Martina's liver, Isabel's hefty hips, Natasha reading Dostoevsky while I kissed her neck, the other Isabel making love standing in the ocean, Veronica with her velvety pubis, little Linda with her spasm-inducing orgasms, all the women I have ever looked in the eye, all the women who have looked me in the eye, all those bodies I have undressed, all those hands running their fingers through my hair, stroking the small of my neck, my chest, my thighs, my penis. Swedish women sunbathing topless on the beach, with me harbouring an almighty erection above my swimming trunks, and all the others laughing at me as I lay face down on the hot sand: "Hey, Mr. Oilman, let us know when you hit the well, right?"

MNEMOTECHNICS: Light itself does not have any volume. Remember the experiment involving a magnifying glass and some ants? You focus, focus, try to focus all the light into one single point. Yes, the photons can be squeezed together: how many angels of light can dance on a needlepoint?

BABY: Baba baby boo boo!

BACKGROUND_NOISE: It's a fine day, a fine week, a fine month, a fine year. I bite a chunk of juicy happiness every minute of every day.

ALTER_IAGO: It's all so clear. What can you see? Not much farther than the tip of your nose. What can you do? Stuff yourself like a pig, then dig your grave, all teeth and ears and nose and eyes. With every single little hot throb of your hips.

ODOROUS: The scent of the lilac grove, the salty tang of mornings at the seaside, the smell of roasted chestnuts and fresh-fallen snow, the tarry smell of the freight trains, the nutty smell of white wood, the smell of rosin, the smell of steam in a Turkish bath, the smell of horse sweat and that of ancient tomes.

DADA: executions
                    fingerprints and shipwrecks
                                            warranties, waterfalls
            imitations
rainbows, clouds   raffle
                    premonition, resentment
            evasions, curses,
                                    swamps, slides
                spiderwebs,   tears,
                                                tautology,
            magic tricks,   soap bubbles
                    paper boats, butterflies
flags,
                    flames, sparks and ashes in urns

FLY_IN_JAR: The man with eleven dimensions: heat, pressure, cold, color, shape, sound, dizziness, smell, taste, full and empty—a Golem made up of sensations, emotions, feelings, imagination, will and memory. A rotating sphere constantly battered by impulses and constantly emitting responses. Hyperspace of abstract vibrations. At its very core, the heart of your mind throbs, that very soulful essence of your being. Infinitely present, right here, right now!

PAVLOV'S_DOG: I can see clearly now the fleas have gone… Or so I thought!

MNEMOTECHNICS: OK, take one gene, the one that encodes spiderosis, a protein that controls the flexibility and elasticity of the spider's thread, far more resilient than the toughest steel, and introduce it into a goat's genome. Then milk that goat and make cheese. That cheese will be an excellent insulator, representing the building materials of the future.

LADYD: I collect victories, passions, disappointments, failures, illusions, anxieties, submissions, hopes, regrets… for further information, please contact me at the following address: ladyd@nevermore.com

ALTER_IAGO: Of course we all know what the final destination is: yep, we're all heading towards death, so we all have a fixed target, a precise goal, don't we, a democratic and universal goal. So that's the point that Archimedes was talking about. I talk, you talk, I say something, you answer, we are connected through a cable of spaghetti words which feeds our illusions, yet they too will end up blowing in the wind like dandelion puffs.

GOURMANDE: Bitterness, you can spot bitterness in almost anything.

ONIRIKON: This morning I realized that, when I am dreaming, I can see the world from many different angles simultaneously. I was a pupil in primary school, they were checking our uniforms. When it was my turn in front of the teacher, a tall lady with glasses and her hair in a bun, she scolded me for not having a tie. I could watch myself from the front, in my T-shirt. I had just come back from playing basketball, and had tucked my shirt and tie into my schoolbag. Then I saw myself simultaneously from the back. I had a crew cut, all shaved round the neck, and on the left-hand side, I had a small red mole, like a baby ladybird ready to fly. *Ladybird, ladybird, fly away home...*

BACKGROUND_NOISE: It's a fine day, a fine week, a fine month, a fine year. I bite a chunk of juicy happiness every minute of every day.

ODOROUS: The smell of freshly churned cheese, of grape pulp, of hot metal and pine sap, the scent of myrrh, of lavender fields, of spring showers, of linden leaves, the aroma of quince, of fresh cow's milk, the smell of patience plant, of mothballs and kerosene, of turpentine and glue, the aroma of orange blossoms, fermenting grape juice and freshly baked bread.

DADA: islands, promontories and estuaries, syncopation, rejection, hesitation,
comets, planets, giraffes and graffiti, oddities, ironies,
moguls, slaloms, hopscotch, charade, parade,
dead ends, coquettishness, grinning, crutches, neon lights,
masks, platypus, fire extinguishers,
fission, fusion, umbilical cords,
eyelids and blinks,

corridas,
copulation, snowfall,
harvest, farcical, etymology,
frissons, photos, delirious, avalanches,
declaration, revolution, nightmares, advertisements
auctions, short circuits, freefalls, all of these moments
eternally tattooed…

COCKADOODLEDOO: Cockadoodledoo!

PAVLOV'S_DOG: Impertinent boy, get out of my class this very instant! And bring your parents to school tomorrow!

DADA: All these moments eternally tattooed in my thoughts, fragmented, piecemeal ideas, at the intersection of emotion, impulse and restraint, all these moments flying over one another, merging, swooping, in the cocktail shaker cup of my brain. Light gets drawn on the retina of my window, the window opens in my head, thoughts take flight like a buzzing swarm of bees. I surf on the crest of time like a skydiver on a breath of wind, unmoved in the eye of the storm. I say I am, and instantly realize that I am using the wrong tense, yet this constant error gives me the illusion of profound causality. It's precisely in this pining for coherence, and, at the same time, suppressing any form of nostalgia, that I find my question/answer: to be *and* not to be.

JELLO: I've said it a thousand times. Opposites attract. When I touch something boiling hot or something icy, it bloody well hurts just the same.

BACKGROUND_NOISE: It's a fine day…

The discussions on the Pessoa e-group carried on through-out the spring and then the whole summer, with me only occasionally sleeping at home. I had bought a laptop with a satellite and Wifi connection and I could now log onto the Internet even while I was on the bus or the toilet. The first thing I would do when I woke up in the morning was to check my email and then post a new message on the e-group site. Sometimes I'd do that even before brushing my teeth.

Summer is a great time for investments. People are on vacation. They've got time to dream. Permutations of six by six: classic cars, country homes, yachts, planes, traveling... all of this, of course, once they had seen their kids graduate from Harvard or Yale. Our agents sell these guys all sorts of fantasy plans for their retirement. When it's real hot outside, imaginations run wild and pockets run dry.

I was working nearly every weekend, and all my spare time I would spend on my discussion groups. The game of being myself had become addictive. My colleagues eyed me with suspicion.

"Hi!" "Hi there!" "How are you?" "Fine, and you?" "Fine." "Bye then." "Bye." That was about it, as far as our social con-versations went. My professional commitment hadn't gone unnoticed at the senior level. I was held up as an example of dedication to the firm. They gave me a raise, were about to promote me to quant manager level.

On the other hand, however, the more I worked after hours, the more the number of participants in the Pessoa e-group increased. The relationships between all of them became more and more complex. My mind felt like a ter-mite mound, discovering new layers and channels every day. This process of pixelization seemed endless. I could gener-ate email addresses as frenetically as Chaplin could work the screws in *Modern Times.* Every tendency, every tiny gesture would immediately result in a new character, with a distinct name. The discussions between the different characters were becoming shorter and shorter, sometimes no more than simple interjections or onomatopoeia. Then suddenly, when the number of email addresses had passed several hundred, there was a radical shift. Every word of every message became characters in their own right. Concepts, notions, abstract categories—they all vanished. Level zero. Mental shorthand. I could communicate now in a sort of proto-Chinese without verbs, conjunctions or prepositions. Every word was a proper noun. I could only think in capital letters. Every word/character had the right to speak up in this absolute democracy. Dialogue had turned into a domino game: once a word was uttered, the word/character would add a new loop to the message chain. And so on and so forth.

I found it more and more difficult to stick to my calculations. There were times when even the simplest arithmetic seemed to stump me. How can two and two equal four, when only a single "Two" is worthy of such a designation?

The week after Labor Day, I only slept at home for about two nights and worked all weekend. Monday evening at 10:30, with a final burst of effort, I managed to finish the project for the next day's deadline and then logged onto the Pessoa group. I only slept about one hour that night. The next day, at a quarter to nine, when the first plane hit the tower, I was on the Internet. A robotic voice told us not to panic. "Please remain seated. Do not leave the building, nothing is happening." The tower shuddered, but I told myself there was no point in losing my cool. The modem had gone down, but I managed to reconnect to the Internet using the satellite connection on my laptop. When the second plane hit the other tower, and the second explosion detonated, I do remember hearing some screams. I had another three hours before I had to hand in my project, so I continued my solitary game. When the South Tower collapsed, in the quake that followed, the cubicle walls came crashing down. The whole room was full of dust and glass shards. I stood up and looked around me. All my colleagues had left already. I closed my laptop, took it under my arm and went out into the hallway. I called for the elevator. Of the eight elevators, only three were still working. The doors opened on one. There were two women inside, faces all twisted in fear. I got in. The elevator started moving. The women were silent. Suddenly, the elevator stopped. The numbers above the door showed us we were on the ninth floor. I pressed various buttons, but to no avail. The elevator stayed put. I pushed the red alarm button and said: "No Panic. Help Button." The older of the women, a plump redhead, shrieked at me: "God, listen to him, we're stuck in the elevator with a robot! Hey, Mr. ET, you got any idea what's going on? Haven't you seen the South Tower falling? If we don't get out of here at once, we're screwed!"

The other woman, a short brunette, started weeping. I pushed the button to open the doors. They half-did. There was a gray wall in front of us. We were stuck between floors. The redhead started yelling hysterically: "Help, help! Get us out of here!" She threw herself at the wall and scratched it desperately with her nails. The brunette took off her shoes and started hitting the wall with the heels. The stiletto heels left little round marks on the wall. The redhead said: "What are you looking at? Give me your laptop!" "Connection Failure. Screening."

The woman looked at me with pity. "You think we have time to connect now?" I handed her my laptop. She took it with both hands, lifted it above her head and slammed it against the wall with all her might. The laptop smashed to pieces, leaving a hole in the wall about the size of a tennis ball. "You're not going to cry, are you?" I didn't answer. It was all a bad dream. Why the hell couldn't I wake up? The alarm must have been switched off or something? Urged on by the two women, I took off my sneakers and started chipping at some ebonite to enlarge the hole. In a quarter of an hour, we were all on the ninth floor. The elevators weren't working at all now, and, anyway, we had no intention of getting into one again. I opened a door marked "Exit." The emergency lighting was on. We went down the stairs, full of people who were literally howling. For the first time, I felt scared. I felt my facial muscles getting rigid, and my hairs really did stand on end. All those pieces of the jigsaw that I'd been playing with earlier had blown away like autumn leaves. What was happening to me? What was happening with the world? Where was I? Is this what the Apocalypse looks like?

I went down those stairs, pushed by the people behind me. On the ground floor, the lobby was full of thick smoke, making me choke. There was a horrible stench of burnt plastic and human flesh. My eyes were watering. I was coughing. I threw up a couple of times. I was about to pass out, when someone grabbed my arm. The man who dragged me outside had a fire-fighter helmet on, with a light on top of it. When I got outside, he pointed and said: "Run that way! Run." I turned to thank him, but he was already back inside the building. I started running through the thick smog. Less than a minute later, an almighty crash nearly broke my eardrums. The shockwave hurled me to the ground and a tree branch fell on my left leg.

It's been nearly two years now. When I stand for any length of time my knee hurts. The surgeons did a good job, but any ligament transplant is a bit like a second-hand car: you never know when it will let you down.

A week after surgery, I was released from hospital. There were only three words left on the screensaver of my brain: "Run that way!" I could hear people talking, but their voices just disappeared into the black hole that had replaced my mind. I was an empty shell abandoned by a runaway snail. Owing to lack of activity, the Pessoa e-group and all the hundreds of email addresses were deleted by the administrators.

Without Kimba I would still be a zombie now. Kimba is an Alsatian, with long, attentive ears. Quiet, intelligent, sensitive. Kimba can't talk, but his look says more than a thousand words. In that moment, I was lost, gazing forlornly ahead, arms limp by my side. The dog came close, stuck his muzzle in my left hand and licked me. I started crying. I was in a tent, surrounded by medical staff, police, firefighters and dogs especially trained to deal with those in a severe state of shock. I stroked his head. Kimba barked. Just once.

I went outside. I was on the left bank of the Hudson. Across the river there were some wispy strands of fog. The Colgate clock showed a quarter past five. The West Highway was chock-a-block with trucks and diggers, leaving filled with people dressed in overalls, coming back with broken steel and debris. On the sidewalks, passers-by encouraged them. Flags, honks, clapping. The leaves on the trees were covered in fine ash-colored dust. I looked down toward the tip of Manhattan. A huge cloud of smoke snaked its way up among the skyscrapers. The Statue of Liberty was still there. From where I was standing, it looked a forlorn little toy soldier. I headed for the quay and sat down on a bench facing the river. For months on end, I had been sitting in front of a screen, lost among equations and hundreds of possible combinations in a crazy kaleidoscope. Suddenly, all this e-Babel collapses. The counter goes back to zero. *Press reset and start.* I looked at the green-ish-brown waters of the river. Above the Hudson a flock of pigeons did an unexpected U-turn, their wings glinting in the sun for a mere second. The breeze brought with it the smell of burnt cables. An ambulance siren pierced the air. Life is the strongest drug of all.

A month or so later, I was invited on a TV program, together with Mary-Jane and Emma, the two women in the elevator, to tell audiences how to get out of an elevator using stilettos, a laptop and sneakers. The program was aired again on *Discovery*, you may have seen it yourself. The engineers who had built the walls in the elevator shaft were a bit upset, but we were profoundly grateful to them for building such thin walls. Another two or three inches and we would have been goners, for sure.

The NY Fire Department is organized into 9 divisions, 49 battalions, 203 fire-engines, 143 ladders, 5 help units, 7 squad-rons, 3 marine units, one explosives specialist unit and several other specialized services.

I keep trying to remember some detail that will help me identify my saviour.

The tip of the island is under the remit of Battalion 1, with four fire-engines and three trucks. It was the first unit I visited. Then I went to see the "Tigers," as Unit 6 likes to call itself, then the "Stately Duane Manor," then "Ten House," then "Wall Street" and finally all the other fire-fighting units in South

Manhattan. All of them had lost one or more brothers, as they call their colleagues. When I popped the question, they shrugged despondently: "It could be any one of us!"

That morning of September 11, 2001, 343 fire-fighters died at the World Trade Center. I have looked at their pictures so many times, I have repeated their names over and over again, so much in fact, that I have the list down by heart. 343 words in a dead language.

Joseph Agnello, Brian Ahearn, Eric Allen, Richard Allen, James Amato, Callixto Anaya Jr., Joseph Angelini, Joseph Angelini Jr., Faustino Apostol, David Arce, Louis Arena, Carl Asaro, Gregg Atlas, Gerald Atwood, Gerald Baptiste, Gerard Barbara, Matthew Barnes, Arthur Barry, Steven Bates, Carl Bedigian, Stephen Belson, John Bergin, Paul Beyer, Peter Bielfeld, Brian Bilcher, Carl Bini, Christopher Blackwell, Michael Bocchino, Frank Bonomo, Gary Box, Michael Boyle, Kevin Bracken, Michael Brennan, Peter Brennan, Daniel Brethel, Patrick Brown, Andrew Brunn, Vincent Brunton, Ronald Bucca, Greg Buck, William Burke Jr., Donald Burns, John Burnside, Thomas Butler, Patrick Byrne, George Cain, Salvatore Calabro, Frank Callahan, Michael Cammarata, Brian Cannizzaro, Dennis Carey, Michael Carlo, Michael Carroll, Peter Carroll, Thomas Casoria, Michael Cawley, Vernon Cherry, Nicholas Chiofalo, John Chipura, Michael Clarke, Steven Coakley, Tarel Coleman, John Collins, Robert Cordice, Ruben Correa, James Coyle, Robert Crawford, John Crisci, Dennis Cross, Thomas Cullen III, Robert Curatolo, Edward D'Atri, Michael D'Auria, Scott Davidson, Edward Day, Thomas DeAngelis, Manuel Delvalle, Martin DeMeo, David DeRubbio, Andrew Desperito, Dennis Devlin, Gerard Dewan, George DiPasquale, Kevin Donnelly, Kevin Dowdell, Raymond Downey, Gerard

Duffy, Martin Egan, Michael Elferis, Francis Esposito, Michael
Esposito, Robert Evans, John Fanning, Thomas Farino, Ter-
rence Farrell, Joseph Farrelly, William Feehan, Lee Fehling,
Alan Feinberg, Michael Fiore, John Fischer, Andre Fletcher,
John Florio, Michael Fodor, Thomas Foley, David Fontana,
Robert Foti, Andrew Fredericks, Peter Freund, Thomas Gam-
bino Jr., Peter Ganci Jr., Charles Garbarini, Thomas Gardner,
Matthew Garvey, Bruce Gary, Gary Geidel, Edward Ger-
aghty, Dennis Germain, Vincent Giammona, James Giberson,
Ronnie Gies, Paul Gill, John Ginley, Jeffrey Giordano, John
Giordano, Keith Glascoe, James Gray, Joseph Grzelak, Jose
Guadalupe, Geoffrey Guja, Joseph Gullickson, David Hal-
derman, Vincent Halloran, Robert Hamilton, Sean Hanley,
Thomas Hannafin, Dana Hannon, Daniel Harlin, Harvey
Harrell, Stephen Harrell, Thomas Haskell, Timothy Haskell,
Terence Hatton, Michael Haub, Michael Healey, John Hef-
ferman, Ronnie Henderson, Joseph Henry, William Henry,
Thomas Hetzel, Brian Hickey, Timothy Higgins, Jonathan
Hohmann, Thomas Holohan, Joseph Hunter, Walter Hynes,
Jonathan Ielpi, Frederick J. III Jr., William Johnston, Andrew
Jordan, Karl Joseph, Anthony Jovic, Angel Juarbe, Mychal
Judge, Vincent Kane, Charles Kasper, Paul Keating, Richard
Kelly Jr., Thomas R. Kelly, Thomas W. Kelly, Thomas Ken-
nedy, Ronald Kerwin, Michael Kiefer, Robert King Jr., Scott
Kopytko, William Krukowski, Kenneth Kumpel, Thomas
Kuveikis, David LaForge, William Lake, Robert Lane, Peter
Langone, Scott Larsen, Joseph Leavey, Neil Leavy, Daniel
Libretti, Carlos Lillo, Robert Linnane, Michael Lynch, Michael
Lynch, Michael Lyons, Patrick Lyons, Joseph Maffeo, William
Mahoney, Joseph Maloney, Joseph Marchbanks Jr., Charles
Margiotta, Kenneth Marino, John Marshall, Peter Martin, Paul

Martini, Joseph Mascali, Keithroy Maynard, Brian McAleese, John McAvoy, Thomas McCann, William McGinn, William McGovern, Dennis McHugh, Robert McMahon, Robert McPadden, Terence McShane, Timothy McSweeney, Martin McWilliams, Raymond Meisenheimer, Charles Mendez, Steve Mercado, Douglas Miller, Henry Miller Jr., Robert Minara, Thomas Mingione, Paul Mitchell, Louis Modafferi, Dennis Mojica, Manuel Mojica, Carl Molinaro, Michael Montesi, Thomas Moody, John Moran, Vincent Morello, Christopher Mozzillo, Richard Muldowney Jr., Michael Mullan, Dennis Mulligan, Raymond Murphy, Robert Nagel, John Napolitano, Peter Nelson, Gerard Nevins, Dennis O'Berg, Daniel O'Callaghan, Douglas Oelschlager, Joseph Ogren, Thomas O'Hagan, Samuel Oitice, Patrick O'Keefe, William O'Keefe, Eric Olsen, Jeffery Olsen, Steven Olson, Kevin O'Rourke, Michael Otten, Jeffery Palazzo, Orio Palmer, Frank Palombo, Paul Pansini, John Paolillo, James Pappageorge, Robert Parro, Durrell Pearsall, Glenn Perry, Philip Petti, Kevin Pfeifer, Kenneth Phelan, Christopher Pickford, Shawn Powell, Vincent Princiotta, Kevin Prior, Richard Prunty, Lincoln Quappe, Michael Quilty, Ricardo Quinn, Leonard Ragaglia, Michael Ragusa, Edward Rall, Adam Rand, Donald Regan, Robert Regan, Christian Regenhard, Kevin Reilly, Vernon Richard, James Riches, Joseph Rivelli, Michael Roberts, Michael E. Roberts, Anthony Rodriguez, Matthew Rogan, Nicholas Rossomando, Paul Ruback, Stephen Russell, Michael Russo, Matthew Ryan, Thomas Sabella, Christopher Santora, John Santore, Gregory Saucedo, Dennis Scauso, John Schardt, Fred Scheffold, Thomas Schoales, Gerard Schrang, Gregory Sikorsky, Stephen Siller, Stanley Smagala Jr., Kevin Smith, Leon Smith Jr., Robert Spear Jr., Joseph Spor, Lawrence Stack,

Timothy Stackpole, Gregory Stajk, Jeffery Stark, Benjamin Suarez, Daniel Suhr, Christopher Sullivan, Brian Sweeney, Sean Tallon, Allan Tarasiewicz, Paul Tegtmeier, John Tierney, John Tipping II, Hector Tirado Jr., Richard Van Hine, Peter Vega, Lawrence Veling, John Vigiano II, Sergio Villanueva, Lawrence Virgilio, Robert Wallace, Jeffery Walz, Michael Warchola, Patrick Waters, Kenneth Watson, Michael Weinberg, David Weiss, Timothy Welty, Eugene Whelan, Edward White, Mark Whitford, Glenn Wilkinson, John Williamson, David Wooley, Raymond York.

Reciting these names of dead fire-fighters is my way of praying. I will never find out to whom I owe my life. My memory, however, keeps them all safely engraved like the marble slab on a monument outside some small-town station. It's the monument that only appears on tourist photos because they had a few pictures left on their film. A list of names that no one ever bothers to read.

Compared to my imagination whimsically generating tens and hundreds of distinct characters, the number of heteronyms of the Unknown Hero must be infinite. History plagued by the Pessoa syndrome. History's great road roller: so generous to those who commit atrocities, while the names of the victims are nothing more than common nouns. Lists, archives, plaques, all will turn to dust. Sooner or later, even the memory of the heroic deeds of these brave people will disappear as well, without trace. Just like the messages I used to throw into the endless ocean of solitude that is the Internet, from my tower at the tip of an island.

Digital Dreams

I've been having the same nightmare for three weeks now. I'm in a dark building with light trickling in through high, dusty windows. I'm walking down an ochre-colored corridor. Doors line either side of the corridors, with "Salon 1," "Salon 5" written on some of them. The others have long lost their nameplates. The floor is covered in faded green linoleum.

I open one of the doors at random. There are six metallic beds inside. I notice that only three of them are occupied by some women in pyjamas and dressing-gowns. One of them barks at me in an unknown dialect: "*Ce cauți, domnule, aici?*"

I close the door carefully and make my way down the corridor. Then I suddenly realise in horror that I don't know who I am or what I am doing there. I am completely confused. I don't understand anything. I look for a mirror. Down in the corners I notice some black insects crawling around. I hear running water. I go into a room marked "*Toaletă femei.*"

Water is running in a large, cracked basin. In one corner, there's a chewed-up brush and dust-pan. No mirror anywhere. I head back. At the end of the corridor, some steps lead to a door. I open it and step out into a courtyard. Some skinny and dirty dogs of dubious parentage are lying there. One of them yawns. I notice some buzzing insects whizzing around. I push onwards.

The pavement is cracked in several places. It's very hot. I look over my shoulder. The sign on the building says: "*Spital.*" The buzzing insects are still following me. An alarm-clock rings somewhere. I mutter something and turn over.

The feeling of alienation persists for a few seconds. Who am I? Yes, who am I? *Who are you?* Well, who am I? Of course, I know who I am. I am Dr. Sunshine, specialist in artificial organ transplants. *In a cyberworld, go to the best cyborg doctor...* Who doesn't know Dr. Sunshine? I've got my ads even on the air trains.

This dream is starting to annoy me. I stretch my right hand towards my bed top and go on the Internet. I run a search and discover that the town I was dreaming about is Bucharest, Romania, a country in old Europe—you know, that continent beyond the ocean that decided to unite and become the United States of Europe around 80 years ago. And "*spital,*" "*salon,*" "*toaletă femei*" and "*ce cauți, domnule aici*?" (or "whatcha looking for, mister?") were words in the language spoken in that region.

A hospital in Bucharest? Romania? Europe? How on could I dream something so baroque? What possible connection could there be between Dr. Sunshine and all of this? Maybe I was having a nervous breakdown? What puzzled me most were those insects. For over 50 years now most of the insects had been eradicated, to avoid spreading infectious diseases. Insects... what a strange notion... I searched on the Internet again and discovered the insects that were bugging me in my sleep were called flies.

The domestic fly: **PHYLUM ARHROPODA**, *insect species,* DIPTERA *sub-species,* MUSCIDAE *family, genus* 'FLY'. *Two wings, six legs. Adults live between 15 and 25 days. The domestic fly is 6-7 mm long, the female is larger than the male. It has red eyes and four black narrow stripes on its thorax, making it easily recognizable. Gender distinction is easy, because the female has double the distance between her eyes than the male. The female typically mates only once, while the male is more promiscuous. During copulation, the wings of the male tear at the edges while fighting the females who turn them down. The reproductive potential of the fly is huge, though fortunately it has never been fully implemented. It is estimated that a couple of flies that start to mate in April could, theoretically, by August, have given rise to 191,010,000,000,000,000,000 flies, if all of their offspring survive.*

It was May. If I pressed the sound button, I could hear their buzzing. I pressed the button. The bedroom filled with that disgusting sound. And then something simply extraordinary happened. I saw a fly whizzing round the room. I rubbed my eyes. The fly was still there, buzzing hither and thither. I disconnected from the insect website, but the buzzing continued. No way I could make it stop. Then I noticed the window was open. "How could I have possibly slept last night with my window open?" But still, a fly in Cyborg Land, that was something! A sensational piece of news! I saw that the fly had settled on the ceiling. I went to the kitchen, got a champagne glass and clamped it over the fly. The fly didn't seem to care. Not a move. I slid the glass on the ceiling right up to the corner. The fly fell into the glass and remained motionless. I took my palm off the glass. Nothing. The fly wasn't moving. Maybe I had stifled it. Maybe it was over-sensitive. Maybe it had experienced a heart attack. Who knows where it had come from? I put it in the palm of my hand and examined it carefully. I don't know why, but I suddenly felt really bad. I couldn't get over the fact that I had committed a terrible crime.

I carefully placed the fly in a little plastic box in which I used to keep my old contact lenses. I have been looking at it three–four times a day. In one week, I had studied all of it. Every single little vein on its wings, every little hair on its legs. My fly was a female, her wings were intact and her eyes wide apart. She had almost certainly been a virgin. When I mentioned that to my psyborg, he immediately declared me (among great gales of laughter) completely mad, but he said that fortunately my madness would dissolve of its own accord, as the fly would soon dry out, fall to pieces and there wouldn't be anything left of it.

I panicked. My fly would disappear. How was that possible?

I phoned the funeral parlors, who at first laughed at me and then gently suggested I should take a long vacation and find myself. I phoned taxidermists but to no avail. I finally found a solution when I discovered the website of an old jeweler who specialised in preserving organic materials in amber.

I went to see him on a Saturday.

He looked at me and asked: "Well, what do you want me to do with this?"

"I would like you to cast it in amber, I read on the Net that you are a specialist in preserving insects with amber."

The old man stared at me over the top of his glasses and answered seriously:

"Never thought I would live to see this. Don't you realise, it would cost you a fortune? Why don't you just change its batteries, it's much cheaper? Just go into the shop next door. This is a new prototype. I believe it won't cost you more than a few cents."

"What do you mean, a new prototype?"

"Well, a prototype, an artificial fly advertising holiday breaks in tropical places. The only place you still find these funny creatures out in the open is in some theme park sponsored by the Green Party. Don't you watch the news? There are fly-adverts all over town at the moment…"

I put my box back in the pocket and left the shop as if remote-controlled.

I haven't got a clue how I made it home. I was shocked. I phoned the people at HQ: "I don't know what's happening to me lately. I have bad dreams, about insects and a town from about a hundred years ago in Romania, you know, in Europe."

"Don't worry, we're onto it. It's this new dream software. We've had a lot of complaints from customers. The software randomly chooses a period and a location from its mainframe databank. You're one of the unlucky ones. Connect to the network. Start Horton Dream Cleaner and select the option *Debug my dreams*. That will solve your nightmare problems. You might not dream for a while, but better no dreams than bad dreams, as they say. These analogical simulations are causing us a bit of a headache."

*

I hang up. Somewhere, I hear someone knocking on the door. I mutter something and this time I really do wake up.

"Doctor, doctor, it's me, Mariana."

"What is it, Mariana, what's up?" I open the door. The nurse looks sheepishly at me. Light barely trickles into the ochre-colored corridor. The door of one of the wards opens with a squeak.

"Well, doctor, you said I should wake you up for the ward rounds."

"Right, Mariana, thanks a lot."

"Sir…"

"What else?"

"You fell asleep with your windows open and you've been bitten by flies."

"Ah, Mariana, what would we do without those flies?"

The Simulator

My love was deep and therefore lasted only the space of one second,
Unable to expand in more than one dimension at a time.
ROSMARIE WALDROP

Several of the Great Programmer's universes will feature another
Great Programmer who programs another Big Computer to run
all possible universes. Obviously, there are infinite chains of Great
Programmers. If our own universe allowed for enough storage, enough
time, and fault-free computing, then you could be one of them.
JUERGEN SCHMIDHUBER

I was sixteen, on vacation with two of my friends in the Bucegi mountains. We were camping and eating sandwiches with cream cheese and red peppers. The air was heavy with the scent of pines; nearby was a stream with icy-clear waters. We would make a fire at night and watch the stars sparkling in the sky. There were so many of them that you could fall asleep counting them.

One night, I dreamt of Einstein. He was wearing a white shirt and a gray woollen vest, with wild hair and bushy eyebrows, and he was using yellow chalk to write some equations on a blackboard, equations which he was explaining to me slowly and emphatically. He spoke a heavily-accented English, rolling his r's. The unified field theory. That bridge between astrophysics and quantum physics, the unifying force behind everything in the universe. In my dream, I felt I understood him. For a couple of moments, the solution seemed at hand.

After graduating from high school, I studied physics at the university, first among peers. I then was awarded a fellowship to the US. Ph.D., post-doc, assistant professor at Stanford... a career progression as steady as a fired bullet. But then, at just under thirty years of age, and already considered one of the bright stars among the physicists of my generation, something happened.

One Sunday morning, instead of jumping out of bed to log onto the computer, I lay back and contemplated the ceiling, thinking of all the work I had done so far. Academia in the US was far removed from the democratic community of kindred spirits, passionate about uncovering the mysteries of the universe—the kind of community I had so sincerely believed in at first. Research quality seemed to be judged solely by the sheer quantity of papers produced and the funding you were able to nail for your projects. The department was paying me to regurgitate other people's theories. Schrödinger's equation, Bohr's model, Kaluza Klein theory. Six leptons and six quarks, eight gluons, four fundamental forces, seven conservation laws. Students would learn to spell out the alphabet diligently: 'b' follows 'a,' 'c' follows 'b.' No asking why and wherefore. Any heresy was instantly decried. I wasn't paid to sow doubts, but certainty. Students expected me to boost their confidence as efficiently as possible. Equations, formulae, laws. I wasn't paid to create anything. I was operating within a system with precise rules. I had chosen physics because I loved it, but now it had just turned into a job. Routine. The same admin hassle, the same endless forms to complete, the same boring funding applications day after day after day. Statistics to show how productive you are, courses you have to do as part of the curriculum, student seminars, run-ins with the head of the department. Ad infinitum. Or the more I thought about it, the more I felt nauseated.

That morning, I finally got it. I was wasting my time. This was not my dream. Less than a week later, after another night of deep thought fuelled by a gin bottle, I jumped ship. After seven years at Stanford, I left my academic career and went to Canada. I spent a few months looking for work, living off my savings and some social handouts. Then I drifted through a series of temporary jobs, until I was hired to work part-time in a company handling the purchasing and distribution of maple syrup. A perfect job. I had enough money, but most importantly, I had lots of spare time to continue my research into theoretical physics.

When I was just a kid, Einstein had given me the best present ever. Thanks to him, I had discovered that secret lab where I could access any experiment at any time of day or night. That ideal lab, that geometrical locus of all my fantasies: my mind. In the States, I had been hibernating, but in Canada my enthusiasm started flowing once more. I had started asking questions once again, working on problems that had preoc-cupied me at university. Oxygen. Canada is a country full of oxygen. In Canada, I felt I could breathe again.

I am walking down the street. Gusts of wind slash across the solid curtain of snow, laying bare small fragments of build-ings. Montreal. Snow, whirling flakes, people bundled up in clothes, woolly or fur hats on their heads. It's March. Where do I begin? The wind, for example. Or time. Maybe time is like the wind, with variable intensity, at times flowing slowly, at times faster, in gusts. Pulsating time, like a heartbeat. Bradycardia, tachycardia. Multidimensional time curled up like a knot of snakes, vertical time springing up like a geyser, time to digest and time to double the population of China. Time to blink and time to let the mulberries ripen. Time to breathe out and time for the solar eclipse in New Guinea. Time to watch your nails grow, time for an empire to fall. You cross the street and at the same time, across the world, there are millions of people crossing other streets. You dream and there are millions of other people dreaming with you. Accidents. Fractures. Not a continual flow, but jumps, lulls, sudden changes of direction. Without them there would be no beginning. There is no beginning. Just some unanswered questions. You can start anywhere. We don't know the answers to the fundamental questions. All we can do is predict.

At the beginning of the twentieth century, Einstein introduced non-Euclidean geometry to describe space. The logic followed by physicists, however, remains bivalent. Experiments in quantum mechanics are still interpreted according to Boolean logic. Until recently, polyvalent logic was just a fad for Ph.D. students in Maths to impress and pull first-year Physics undergraduates. Cocktail chatter. Łukasiewicz, Bocivar, Heyting. Only in the past ten years or so have physicists started taking this seriously and including polyvalent logic in their models.

It's snowing and the blanket of snow is fragmenting the city into thousands of amniotic islands through which cars and people glide in staccato motion, like on a scratched DVD. An ambulance siren screams past me. Cars stop to let it go by. The sound fades into the distance. Doppler's Effect. Or, since we are in Montreal, Fizeau's Effect. I am walking down the street and my body is tracing an undulatory trajectory in space and time, pulled hither and thither by the wind. I am thinking, but my thoughts jump from here to there like a child playing hopscotch.

Initially, in his theory of special relativity, Einstein demonstrated that mass can convert to energy. Then, in the general theory of relativity, he went further and claimed that the very geometry of space-time can influence matter. Gravity, he told us, is a sort of crease in the geometrical structure of space-time. From that time onwards, geometry, matter and fields can all be regarded as different forms of the same fundamental "substance."

Gray buildings. Parallelepipeds. Structures at all levels, from democratically distributed quarks, three on each particle, up to the beautifully aligned galaxies, like dewdrops clinging to the invisible threads of some cosmic spiderweb. The structure of our mind contemplating the structure of the world. Mirrors. Symmetry. As Kant observed, our minds are constructed in such a way that we see relationships and structures everywhere, so it's very hard to distinguish between our own internal coherence of reality and the coherence we seek to impose on it. Like Baron Münchhausen, we keep trying to pull ourselves, and even our horse, out of the swamp by our hair, only to end up bald.

Together, the standard quantum model and the theory of gravity describe all of the phenomena of the world we currently know. Unfortunately, the two models are incompatible. We have to find some kind of common language in which the two dialects can coexist and talk to each other, in order to find the equations of the unified field theory. Theoretically, there are three ways in which you can unify the models a and b:

~ you can translate a into b
~ you can find a more encompassing model c in which a and b can be subcomponents
~ you prove that one of them is false.

At the logical level, you can invent a non-dual logic that gives up on the principle of identity, suggesting instead the existence of elements that are simultaneously distinct and respectively identical with themselves. At the algebraic level, you can introduce structures that are concurrently discrete yet continuous. At the geometric level, you can build a non-commutative space where the Minkovski/Riemann structures would be special cases. But that's not the kind of unification we need. We need to find a theory that will predict the granularity of space, different forces at different levels, and the existence of elementary particles. A theory that can predict things, not sterile word games.

The model I had been working on since coming to Canada, that huge universal grid, was not composed of strings of nine or ten dimensions, as in string theory, but some sort of system in which neural networks communicate with each other. Over and above Einstein's model, mine took into account information theory. The universe isn't a clockwork mechanism that stops if you forget to wind it. The universe isn't an engine for producing entropy. The universe is a giant brain generating the history of the cosmos. This brain does not have a single central unit like an ordinary computer, but billions and billions of central units working simultaneously. Like a swarm of bees. Or a termite mountain.

The one fundamental thing is neither matter nor fields nor space-time geometry. Instead, it's the exchange of information.

"It from bit," as Wheeler had suspected. Just like our own brain creates a unique picture of the universe, so the universe-brain generates a unique reality in which we live. Space-time exists so that information can be processed. "To be" means "to be connected." The universe is a giant information processor, a sort of cosmic internet. A universal translator in which there is continual simultaneous interpretation between the analogue and the digital levels of the world. The speed of light may represent the limits of movement, but not of communication. In other words, nothing can *physically* exceed the speed of light, but information can move *virtually* at speeds beyond that of light.

One of my working hypotheses was that the fluctuation of black holes allows mathematical operations that are much faster than the speed of light. We humans use grammar as well as logic to make sense of the world. And the universe is a mind, a gigantic mind, a mind generating language-like structures. Its rules are grammatical rules.

It is very difficult to do complex calculations without using the computer. Or, to be precise, computers, for a single one would not be enough. Last year, I'd taken part in the auctioning of assets from an investment company that had gone bust. I'd managed to acquire 49 top-flight computers for next to nothing. Each one had more than two thousand terabytes of memory. A fluke. And the attic I had crammed them into had all the potential to be the backdrop for the next film in the *Matrix* series, albeit the paleobyte version.

For my simulations, I was using a software program for neural networks. First, I would feed the networks with information: equations, formulae, calculations, results published in the journals of Geneva's CERN and Chicago's Fermilab particle accelerators, results from the telescopes of Mauna Kea, Hawaii and the NASA satellites and space probes, anything that could have even the remotest connection with the unified Theory of Everything, as my pompous physicist colleagues had called it. I would then generate families of models that I would test, getting them to predict various constants or physical values that have been tested experimentally, so as to verify the equations. Since Gödel, we know that it is impossible to prove every single proposition in a complete axiomatic system. Starting from the experimental data, the neural networks could create a minimal set of equations whose predictions could be instantly verified. In order to avoid the dead road of Gödel's incompleteness theorem, I would manually add the equations in which there was a physical value that could not be deduced from this minimal set of equations. The neural networks generated forms, not only forms of solutions, but also forms of rational thought patterns. These rational forms were continually evolving through natural selection, which increased their descriptive power exponentially.

A network with three neural levels can already solve complicated functions. However, to combine all of the parameters of the physical world, you needed complex neural architecture, connected in parallel to form metaneural networks, which in turn would be connected to metametaneural networks, and so on, until we got to a superstructure on six levels. The architecture of the digital neurons simulated the human cortex, organised into different areas with different functions. The 49 computers were working non-stop. A former hacker from California had the idea to use the Internet to simultaneously process real-time data and had created the company Zettabyte. For a monthly fee, you could access their network of computers for your scientific or artistic projects. The processing power of these millions of parallel servers was incredible, a thousand times greater than that of the MareNostrum computer installed in a disused chapel on the campus of the Catalan Polytechnical Institute in Barcelona, or the BlueGene architecture envisioned by IBM. However, bearing in mind that the rapport between Planck's units and the diameter of the universe was 10 to the power of 61, even with the help of Zettabyte, the simulations could take weeks. When I was out of town, I would watch over things remotely, through my laptop, check the results and restart the programs. It was like fishing. You need to be very patient.

Snowflakes float through the air, drawing the force lines of the gravitational field. I head for the metro station, thinking of my most recent results. Snow, wind, cold simply don't exist for me. In my mind's eye, atmospheric conditions are always ideal and constant. I walk down the stairs. Two beggars hold the door open for me and wish me a good day. They are dressed in blue jackets and fur hats with flaps over their ears. Both of them have red faces and hoarse voices. They stink of alcohol. Their faces are screwed up and the wind makes them blink rapidly. Absent-mindedly, I search my pockets for some change.

Until Copernicus, people thought that our good Earth was the belly button of the universe. Then, when they managed to see a little bit beyond the end of their noses, they moved the sun to the center. Now we know that our sun is an absolutely mediocre star not that different from tens of billions of other stars in our galaxy, which in turn is lost among a hundred billion other galaxies. Far from being in the center of our galaxy, more than thirty thousand light years separate our sun from the galaxy's midpoint. And then, most of the mass in the universe is invisible. The list of ingredients for our universe? 73% dark energy. 23% dark matter. 4%—the absolute minority—are stars, planets and other baryonic particles of which we are composed. It's not visible matter that weighs most heavily on the cosmic scales, but that mysterious dark energy, which could be the energy of a vacuum or that quintessential remnant energy of the Big Bang, itself. If indeed there had ever been a Big Bang, because some of the stars in the furthermost galaxies seem to be a good deal older than the 13.7 billion years when the whole circus is supposed to have started. Indeed, it's very clear that given the matter we are made from, we are not only decidedly *not* in the center of the universe, but we are a rare commodity, a little delicacy in the huge cosmic feast.

"Passengers for Quebec City please head to Gate 35." I queue up with the ticket in my hand. It's Friday and the coach is full of commuters heading home. I find a window seat and take a Romanian book out of my backpack, a book about the theory of graphs. I open it up but cannot focus. Words dash about in front of me without making any sense. A smiley, mulatto woman in a green coat sits down next to me. I look at the coach terminal yard through the window, and beyond it, at the whirling curtain of snow, white trees, the outline of squat houses, the heavy, opaque sky.

In the general theory of relativity, the universe has a very clear history without any doubts. "God does not play dice," Einstein warned us. On the other hand, in quantum theory, matter is made up of nothing but fluctuation and uncertainty that limit our ability to measure things, so we can never simultaneously catch the particle and the wave characteristics, as Heisenberg's famous principle states. But even here, space-time continues to be well-defined. In contrast, one of the recent models of TOE even has the architecture of space-time fluctuating, and uncertainty spreads toward space-time as well, so that it becomes a sort of statistical foam, a network of fluctuating relationships. Fundamentally, the world is simultaneous, non-localised. What we perceive as direction, form and sequence is merely the schizophrenic dialogue between observer and the observed object. Thought, itself, gives form and name, time and space to this simultaneous amorphous ocean. On one hand we have that vast reach of potentiality, on the other hand my mind gives birth to words and ideas and therefore their space-time. But it's an artificial distinction, a useless one, since I am part of that vast ocean myself. The structure that generates my thinking is immersed in that—so is that blank spot of my mind which I intuitively know is there but can never perceive directly, since I cannot think my thinking itself, just as I cannot see my sight.

The limitation of any model is that it is an abstract representation of the world. Some elements are taken into account, others are ignored. In an isolated physical system, everything works perfectly. The problem is that in nature there are no isolated systems. For instance, a clock. What is a clock? All the physics books say: "An isolated system is one which periodically reaches the same state. When this cycle is constant, we consider this isolated system to be a clock, by definition." Then Einstein's sleight of hand: "Clocks measure time. Time is what clocks measure." A circular explanation, because even a child can realise that the idea of a clock is absurd when there are no isolated systems. Who has ever seen an isolated physical system?

Physics is incomplete, it doesn't take into account essential things, for the world is not a collection of identical points or homogeneous molecules. We are not robots, and the universe is not a computer. Imagine the very start of things, the Big Bang, when the whole universe was concentrated in a tiny point and then, for some unfathomed reason, a sudden explosion creates the info-geometric matrix of the world, then three seconds later the quarks appear, after hundreds of thousands of years the atoms, and then things slow down, and it will take hundreds of millions of years for the stars, planets and galaxies to appear. Where is that single tiny point now? Because of their common birth, every point in the universe is still connected with every other point in the universe in some mysterious way. In fact, every point in the universe *is* that unique, ubiquitous point from the very birth of the universe. No, the world is not a random collection of elementary particles whirling and spinning, driven by entropy or other blind forces. Our universe is *alive* and all the phenomena are interconnected and co-dependent. Our universe breathes like the oceans on a night with a full moon, our universe is *intelligent*.

The bus crosses the Jacques Cartier Bridge now, heading for Autoroute 20. The St. Laurent River is covered with jagged ice, rather like the planet Krypton after the explosion.

Einstein used mystery to explain another mystery. He's hardly the first, nor the only one to do that. Newton did the same. Up to the Morley-Davidson experiments, all physicists would talk blithely about ether. Now we've all agreed that ether does not exist. Then, we chased after the gravitons predicted by the string theory. Physics is nothing else but the history of fictions first admired, then despised, then abandoned. The Earth is a giant plate sat upon the backs of four elephants who in turn balance on the shell of an enormous tortoise. When the tortoise sneezes, the elephants get tickled, and that's how earthquakes appear. Cartoons and funny stories. Tom and Jerry. The fiction of clock and the ether. The fiction of time. Stories, stories with one, two, three, five or seven characters. Stories. And how do they start? Well, like all stories. Once upon a time there was a Big Bang. Suddenly, out of a tiny point bereft of any dimension, this whole world appears and everything that is in it. Characters? The elementary particles. Scenario? The four fundamental forces. And how did the whole show start? Well, the explosion. And why did the explosion happen? Our explanations? A non-dimensional point and an explosion. A fairy tale with knights and dragons.

We develop global models by generalizing on the basis of local ones. Copy and paste. Copy and paste. Copy and bingo! There comes the blockbuster, that brand new model of the universe. Mental collage. A bit from here, a fragment from there, and then, thanks to the international norms to reduce, reuse, recycle ideas, there we have it, that superb, grandiose comedy.

The whole edifice of science is based upon it being repeatable, upon the exact replication of an experiment. But in reality, nothing cannot be completely replicated. What do we base our generalizations on? Suppositions, hunches, incomplete deductions. Giant soap bubbles, froth. Everything can be reduced to the degree of freedom of our minds. That's the clever bit. How complex and colorful our dreams are. How many different variables we can consider simultaneously, how many independent movements, how many distinct rotational planes we can imagine. Take any theory and you will see that they all have in common some intuitive slogan such as "energy cannot be destroyed"; or "symmetry, symmetry at any price"; the principle of minimum effort and therefore minimal path with a minimal number of independent variables, like energy, mass, dimensions, types of interactions. In the end, all theories dumb down the world to a finite number of relationships, which have nothing to do with the complexity of the world itself, but everything to do with the calculating power of the author of that particular theory. Einstein created at first a model of the world with three degrees of freedom and—presto!—out of the magician's hat popped the famous equation of energy and mass. Then, with a little help from his friend Grossman, he added yet another degree of freedom and—presto!—out popped the equation of general relativity. You take an idea and you generalise it: What if there are space-times in which you cannot rotate objects, in which left and right do not act as mirrors?

And with that simple question, Alain Connes created the whole notion of non-commutative geometry. It's a child's game: Pet et Répète sont dans un bateau; Pet est L'animal est tombée dans l'eau. Qui est reste dans le bateau? Répète… How many degrees of freedom does our universe have fundamentally? Three, four, an infinity? Are space and time derived or non-reductible measurements? Wheeler pointed out that any TOE worth its salt would be a purely algebraic theory. In order to avoid an infinite regression in which every term could only be explained through another term, the unified field theory could not be based on such concepts.

"Could you tell me what language that is, please?" The woman sitting next to me wants to chat. Her hair is dyed red and her eyes are sparkling. She speaks French with a bit of an accent. I put my book back in the bag and answer rather gruffly, since I am not in the mood for chatting: "Romanian, Ma'am. It's a mathematics book. Sorry, but I'm rather tired, I'll have a nap now." And I close my eyes, hoping to be left alone.

Are there any variables and constants in the universe, I wonder? Maybe the laws of nature themselves vary and this variation is unpredictable. We insist on fitting reality into the typecasts of our mind. We juggle with equations, numbers, symbols, representations. Archimedes, Euler, Gauss, Newton, Einstein, Gödel, Feynmann? The master jugglers. Their minds could see all of the variables at once. They could see the solutions. De Broglie talking about the unity of particle and wave, Einstein talking about the curvature of space because of gravity: they created new models to visualise reality. Pure poetry. What did Newton say? *"I do not believe that mathematical units can be broken down into parts however small. Rather, they describe continuous motion. Therefore, units that grow in equal time measures are greater or smaller if they grow at higher or lower velocity."* Intuition: you don't learn such things in school.

Newton's extraordinary discovery was that mathematical symbols are types of movement. Natural numbers describe a different type of movement than irrational numbers. We could classify numbers according to the elementary operations that generated them. For instance, we can imagine rational numbers to be moving in a straight, uniform line, monotonous like the beat of a metronome. The transcendental numbers are generated by a spiral movement with constantly variable acceleration. Imaginary numbers could be the projection of movement from a space with more dimensions. And so on.

But can the world be reduced to numbers? Are numbers, the invention of our Neolithic ancestors, suitable for our world? Kronecker's naivety: *"God created natural numbers. The rest is man's creation."* Two bananas, three oranges, five cucumbers. Classification. What is natural about classification? What is real about a real number? Has anyone seen *pi* in reality?

Maybe the world is fundamentally uncountable. Maybe the world cannot be reduced to mathematical formulae.

Mathematics is based on logic, and the whole scaffolding of logic is based on the three principles of non-contradiction, identity and excluded middle. These three principles derive from our day-to-day experience with objects that have continuity, do not disappear and reappear suddenly, and do not contradict each other continuously. All the complex formulae, all sophisticated equations bear the mark of our daily experience. Even the idea of a function comes from the natural tendency to divide the world into objects and actions. Because that's how the human brain works. The area of the cortex that memorises nouns is different from the area that memorises verbs.

The *a priori* classification of the world in objects and actions is arbitrary. Yes, most languages have both verbs and nouns, but that *doesn't* mean that reality is organised the same way.

Newton in his *Principia Mathematica* and Einstein in his theory of relativity use real numbers. In quantum physics, Bohr and Dirac use complex numbers. Fumbling around for the equations for unified field theory, at some point I had decided to slash the Gordian knot and invent a completely different algebra. Instead of using numbers and operations, I was using a new class of mathematical objects, which I had called "actants," to use a term from Panini's grammar. Actants were simultaneously numbers and operations, functions and variable. The algebra of actants was in that twilight zone at the border of analysis, graph theory, René Thom's semio-topology of catastrophes. In order to be able to work with actants, I had used my neural network to program some subroutines that mimicked the activity of visual receptors. Visual understanding. They could form recognizable shapes from disparate points. Actants were these colored shapes in constant motion. Movies. On the way to discovering TOE, I had started making movies. At Stanford, I had a friend from India who told me about Panini one fine morning, while we were having our tea. Panini was a fascinating creature who had lived in the 5th century B.C. in a small village in northern India and who had been killed by a tiger. He was the author of an extraordinary tome of grammar with a complex system of 3996 intricate rules, the most detailed description ever of any language. To describe the structure of a sentence, or, more generally, to break it down into key components, Panini used six elementary units, which he called "karakas" (actants).

The human cortex also has six layers of neurons, which I thought was more than a simple coincidence. An equation that would start from the base layer of Planck's length would predict the appearance of fundamental forces according to the very texture of that mysterious fundamental substance. And that would indeed be the Great Unification. So, on the first level, it would predict the Higgs force, responsible for the mass of elementary particles; on the second level, the weak interactions; on the third, the strong interactions; on the fourth, electromagnetic forces; on the fifth, gravity; and on the sixth, the super-galactic force of repulsion... The equation to explain the granulation of the world. A hyper-generalised theory of relativity in which we introduce the idea that the world is organised on different levels. The equation that would describe the relationship between energy and structure, and energy and information, referring to structure respectively. The equation that converts energy into information, space-time into structures on specific levels. Six degrees of freedom. Six was my lucky number and, in my simulations to date the hexadic model of the world, produced the most interesting results. In Panini's honor, I had named my network of computers at home after him.

I opened my eyes and looked out of the window. It was still snowing, but a bit more sporadically. We had left the city. There were still white blocks of ice floating on the St. Laurent River, heading for the Atlantic. The landscape was tiring on the eyes. White, white everywhere, different shades and luminosities of white. Suddenly, on the right, a two-humped mountain appeared, looking like a snow-covered mammoth's carcase. Mont St. Hilaire, said a sign on the highway. It was very hot in the bus. I took my laptop out of my bag and checked emails, then connected to the Panini network. The woman next to me had closed her eyes and was listening to music on her iPod.

People read the information bombarding their senses as a continuum. When actually, concepts, abstractions, reflections, thinking itself, reduces and limits and simplifies the world. More than that, the very act of understanding is a substitution, a metaphor. We always understand something through something else. Maybe it's the same thing at the quantum level, maybe there is a more profound analogue level of the world, an ocean of continuous vibration in which the elementary particles are nothing more than digital froth. Or, more likely, as in Chinese philosophy, the two manifestations of matter oscillate between the two states: yin-yang-yin-yang, analogue-digital-analogue-digital...

The white spread outside. Snowflakes clinging to the window. The hum of the engine. Two ladies behind me talking about buying a rug. Most of the passengers are asleep.

The woman beside me has fallen asleep with her mouth open. The contours of her face. The shape of her nose, mouth, chin. What are shapes? The universe as a fundamental state of vibration, the universe as a non-local eternal and ubiquitous fluctuation that keeps changing the states of the spin networks. Cosmic roulette, but in a casino owned by a Mafia boss that fakes the numbers. From Heisenberg onwards, any act of understanding involves an observation that changes reality. We cannot distinguish any more between "being" and "understanding." Shapes depend not only on the phenomenon to be analysed, but also on the one doing the analysis. Which means they are the equations at each level of the forces interacting, of the relationships forming and projecting in front of your very eyes, an expression of energy in equilibrium. Shapes are the visualization of these relationships. The world of shapes is the world of relationship in which objects do not exist. Rainbows. Colored shapes in motion. Actants. Multi-colored Zeppelin. Maybe those guys with the p-branes are right after all, and we are nothing but colored spots on a huge soap bubble. If someone were to pop our bubble… "Hello there!" The woman next to me wakes up and yawns.

She stares at me bewildered. "Are we there already?"

"No, no, plenty of time still, don't worry. What music are you listening to?" I asked politely, checking a text message.

"Not music, I'm listening to the radio. My nephew has recorded through the Internet the radio station from Port-au-Prince. He gave me this machine and the earphones as a Christmas present last year. It helps with the homesickness."

"But the recordings were made some time ago?"

"What does time matter? It's not news I'm interested in, it's important to hear the voices, to feel I am there. In Haiti, time passes far more slowly. Do you know how lovely it is there? If you've never been, you should go. What movie are you watching?" The woman pointed to the screen of my laptop, looking puzzled at the tens of windows I had opened. "Or is that a game? My nephew loves games, can't drag him away from the computer. When I was young, we had other things to do, but now all the young people seem to spend their spare time with their bums on a chair and looking at some screen until their eyes turn red. You're just the same. I've seen your fingers moving on those buttons, like a pianist. You do everything at once—working on the computer, checking messages on your cell phone. It's tiring even to watch you."

I blushed, as if I had been caught red-handed. Doing everything at once. Multitasking, that's what she was referring to. Because the older generation isn't used to that, they think it's exotic. I wasn't aware she had been spying on me.

Initially, in my search for the equation, I had nourished the neural network software with all sorts of data about the universe, measurements taken by spacecrafts and astronomical observatories, satellite images, experimental results from the particle accelerators. At some point, however, I realised that there is no such thing as a magic formula, a unique recipe for baking the cosmic pie, so I adopted a radically different strategy. I no longer tried to deduce all the laws starting from the base level. I understood now that every level of reality had its own laws and I was trying to find the correspondence, the connections between levels that made the existence of the whole structure possible.

My method was neither bottom-up nor top-down, rather, it was starting from an intermediate level in both directions. A kind of jam session. I had evolved from being a physicist, to becoming a composer and movie director. The movies I was directing were in fact database surfing, equations in motion. I smiled, remembering the face the editor made when he received my first article, in which I had inserted a short movie to demonstrate the use of actants in modelling TOE. One of the peer reviewers had been enthusiastic, saying he appreciated my attempts to formalise dual phenomena. The other was very sarcastic, reminding me that Penrose had been working for over 40 years on his twistors and spin networks, without any concrete results besides getting the Nobel prize, while poor Hamilton had died, haunted by the spectre of quaternions. He suggested, only half-jokingly, that I should exhibit my movie in an art gallery. In the end, the article did appear, with minor corrections. Seeing is believing. In the meantime, I had published three more articles, and all of them had a short digital movie attached, at least in the Web version of the publication.

Structures and levels. Considering the succession of Planck length—quarcks—elementary particle—atom—DNA—nucleus—cell—tissue—organism—ecosystem—planet—solar system—galaxy—galactic cluster—supercluster—galaxy filament—the entire universe... the complete matrix string is a structure on 17 levels. The information for the development of an organism is not to be found at a quantum level, but instead at the DNA molecular level. Since an organism is only four levels away from its DNA, it may well be that the information for the development of the universe is not at a quantum level, but at an intermediate level of organization. But which one? A human cell has 46 chromosomes, while the human organism has tens of billions of cells. The number of stars in the universe is estimated to be 10^{24}, so, keeping those proportions going, about ten billion times more than the number of cells in the human body. Accordingly, the human being, who is somewhere halfway between macro- and microcosm, could be a plausible candidate.

"As large as the external space, as vast as all the space that exists is the space inside the heart, for inside you will find everything inseparable, heaven and earth, fire and air, sun and moon, lightning and stars, whatever is here in the world, and whatever is not, whatever has been or will be, all is inseparable here."

My Indian friend from Stanford had given me this sticker with a quote from the *Chandogya Upanishad* and I had stuck it on my fridge. The number of synapses in the human brain is similar to the number of cells in the adult body. The brain has hundreds of thousands of algorithms working in parallel to compute what we call reality. The digital movies that appeared on the screens of my computers up in the loft were also a form of reality that at some point, I hoped, would precisely map the world, a perfect mirror. The demonstration would be that it would be impossible to distinguish between the two. An artificial mind generating the world from bytes. The equation of unified field theory was not a set of formulae, but a Golem.

"No, ma'am, this isn't a movie, nor a game, it's just a program I'm working on."

Then I noticed on her left wrist a bracelet shaped like a bronze snake swallowing its tail. Ouroboros. The Ancient Greeks used it to represent the Milky Way. "If you don't mind my asking, where did you get this bracelet?"

"You like it?" she asked, visibly flattered. "My daughter brought it back as a present from Mexico."

I did a quick search on Wikipedia. Quetzalcoatl. The snake biting its tail was also Aztec. The Greeks had taken it from the Egyptians via the Phoenician route. The Aztecs had probably gotten it from the Toltecs, and they had appropriated it from the Maya. In the meantime, so it wouldn't look as though I was ignoring her, I asked: "How long have you been living in Canada?"

"Three years. My children came here, so I followed them. What can I do, we've got a lot of problems in Haiti."

"Yep, I understand. I'm from Romania and things aren't going too well there either."

"Romania? Hagi's country?"

"What, you know about soccer?"

"It's always been my passion. Pele, Maradona, Vava, Garrincha, Beckenbauer, Platini, Hagi, Baggio, Cruyff, Zidane. These are gods, not humans. Gică Hagi, who doesn't know him?"

"I'm impressed. I have to admit I haven't heard of half of those people. But then I am sure that the names of my 'gods' wouldn't mean much to you either. Have you heard, for example, of Cumrum Vaffa or Alexander Grothendieck?"

"Grothen-what? What kind of a name is that?"

What childishness! What had come over me? Talk about inappropriate response! It's almost like being back at nursery and boasting about your toys. That's all I needed now, to hold a seminar on the bus on quantum gravity or the theory of motives. I was suddenly really sleepy—anything to do with soccer seemed to put me to sleep. Without any further comment, under the pretext that I was exhausted, I closed my eyes.

One of the problems I kept returning to before falling asleep was Cantor's famous theorem. The so-called continuum hypothesis has been a real curse for most mathematicians. Obsessed by it, frustrated by the fact that he could not prove it, Cantor started reading mystical literature and tried to prove that Shakespeare's plays were written by Francis Bacon. Gödel, who was likewise fascinated by this issue, became obsessed by Leibniz and spent many years studying photocopies of his letters, trying to prove that Leibniz's theories were not original. When he was interviewed for American citizenship, Gödel tried to explain to the judge that he had carefully studied the American constitution and that there were some serious flaws in it, which might allow for the appearance of a dictatorship like that of Hitler in Germany. Fortunately, Einstein was present as well, and his prestige helped to save the day. Gödel's citizenship was granted.

In Cantor's relation, $2^{\aleph_0} = c$, where 2 marks the bridge between two infinities, one infinity, (c) is continuous and uncountable, while the other, $\aleph_0$, is discontinuous and countable. This is what the Master had to say about it:

"*If I conceive of infinity in this way, as I have done here and in some of my older attempts, it is because I have a real pleasure, and derive great satisfaction seeing how the whole concept of number, which in finite realm merely has a number background, splits into two concepts once we raise ourselves towards infinity: first, the concept of power, which is independent of the order a set is given; secondly, the concept of number, which is necessarily linked to an order that follows an established law of the set, thus giving the entire set its order. If we descend again from infinity to finity, I can see clearly how the two concepts merge into one, that of the natural finite number.*"

This is a fantastic equivalence between the concept of power and that of number, between simultaneity implied through power, and succession implied through numbers. Continuous—discontinuous, simultaneous—successive, complementary dualities. Cantor's intuition finds an equation for the idea behind Broglie's particle/wave simultaneity. Cantor was the first to see the bridge between the continuous and the discrete world.

At every point in space there is a Big Bang and a Big Crunch. Explosion. Implosion. Every moment the world is created and destroyed. Every point becomes the universe and at every moment the world is teetering on the brink of the void. But there are no points, no moments, it's just a way of talking. The essence of the world is lightning quick, ephemeral, transitory. No points, no moments.

I woke up after the bus entered Quebec City. Although they had sub-zero temperatures outside, the city seemed to exude warmth and comfort. Frontenac Castle, with its red-brick dungeon and cylindrical turrets with cone-shaped roofs and pointy lightning rods, seemed to have come straight out of an Andersen fairy tale. I'd booked a room at a hotel in the Old Town, by the St. Laurent River. On my way there, I entered a bakery and bought myself a baguette with ham and cheese and tomato. The cobblestones gleamed. I was on St. Louis Street, full of tourist-trap restaurants and souvenir shops. Then suddenly, in a shop window, I saw a sculpture made from whalebone, porous and yellow. Some fish, an owl, a bear, a seal, all of these animals hovering above the head of a frightened human figure. In between the animals, the sculptor had scooped out a hole in which he had planted a shiny red foetus with hands folded as if in prayer. At first glance, the various elements of the sculpture seemed to be arranged rather randomly, but if you looked closer, there were strange links between the animals and the humans. Indeed, the whole thing had the coherence of a nightmare. The work of art was entitled "La Creation du Monde" and the artist was Manassie Akpaliapik. The shop window was in fact the Brousseau Inuit Art Gallery of Quebec City. I went in. A tall young man with glasses was at the entrance. I asked him for some details about the artist.

"Manassie Akpaliapik works mostly in fossilised whale bone. You see, whalebones are full of fat, so you need to dry

them out for at least 80 years before you can sculpt them. All
of his works have something disquieting and violent in them.
Manassie is, I suppose, a kind of Van Gogh or Edvard Munch
of Inuit art. He's very popular with collectors. You are lucky
to have seen that work today. A French museum has bought
it and it will be shipped there next week."

The guide showed me an album of Inuit art, which contained other examples of Manassie Akpaliapik's whalebone
creations. I leafed through it. He went on:

"All Inuit art is very recent. Almost everything you see
here was created in the last twenty years. There isn't really an
Inuit style. The artists are all very different. Mattiusi Iyaituk,
for instance, works in the abstract style, like Miro." The guide
showed me a picture with a stone plaque hanging from the
horns of a caribou. "Elisha Sanguya models longish figures
like Giacometti, while Judas Ullulaq's works remind you of
the Cubist paintings of Braque and Picasso. There are however
some artists, such as Nick Sikkuark with his series of animal
and insect spirits, or Maudie Rachel Okittuq with her folkloric
little green men, who are, shall we say, more traditional."

In other words, it's hard to be original nowadays. And yet,
compared to the work in the window, his explanations seemed
ridiculous. *La Création du Monde.* A woman, a child, some
polar animals, a terrified scream. A cruel world, but somehow immaculate. I thanked my guide for his explanations and
left. It was snowing again outside. Place D'Armes was buried
in a blanket of snow. In the center was an ice sculpture of a
bear rising on his hind legs. The lanterns in front of Frontenac
Castle glowed violet. I went down toward Hotel St. Antoine on
the Rue de la Montagne. The hotel reception was a tall room in
rustic style, with beams separating the ground and first floor. I

asked the receptionist if they had any more rooms with a view of the river. The receptionist was young, blonde, with glasses. She had a mole on the left side of her mouth. She smiled.

"You're lucky. Usually, the rooms facing the river are extremely popular, but one has just been vacated. They can't be booked beforehand, so we just allocate them on arrival. The last one is yours!"

I went up in the lift, accompanied by a tall youth who told me his name was George. He was still in high school and only worked at the hotel at the weekend. George also told me that the hotel belonged to one of the wealthiest families in Canada and each room had a different theme. Next time, I should stay in "Le Jardin Bleu." "It's like sleeping on the sea bed." My room was called "Savanne." There was a zebra skin on the wall, and the lamps had orange shades. At first it made for a cozy, intimate atmosphere, but after about five minutes, that red-orange light became tiresome. I left a single bedside lamp on, removed its shade, and plugged in my laptop.

Nothing. Nothing had been caught in my neural network web. On the monitors were chaotic forms that didn't make any sense. As I was too tired to do any more equations, I just went on the Internet and read an article from the latest issue of *Physical Review Letters*. Shortly thereafter, I switched off the laptop and the light and lay down in bed with my eyes open.

There's really only one fundamental issue in physics, forever unresolved: What is time, where does it come from, and where is it going?

Depending on the experiment and the model, space-time can be either continuous or discontinuous. In the theory of relativity, space-time is continuous; in quantum theory it is discontinuous. In the search for TOE, scientists have created either discrete models that quantify physical measures, such as Ashtekar's theory, or continuous models such as the M theory of superstrings in which elementary particles appear as local intensification of the vibratory field of minuscule chords.

According to these theories, time is by turns discrete or continuous. Yet time is the least understood of physical measures. Julian Barbour spent years trying to demonstrate that there is no such thing as time, that what we call time is a fiction created by our brain, which tries to compose a continuous picture and state of being from disparate information that hits us simultaneously. The fundamental laws of quantum physics are symmetrical in time. Yet, in daily life, we never see shards rising up from the ground and reforming into a coffee cup. Penrose thinks there is a secret asymmetry of time at the quantum level that we haven't yet managed to discover. To explain these discrepancies, Prigogine claims that the fundamental laws of physics are actually at a macroscopic level. However, there is another solution, a more radical one. Maybe the very nature of the universe is a paradox. Artificially separated from space, time can only be pure succession, as in Newton's model. In turn, space, when separated from time, becomes absolute simultaneity. But can we have space without time and vice versa?

Einstein told us that time and space cannot be separated, and from then onwards we haven't been able to talk about time or space other than in an arbitrary fashion. This was his best idea (alongside the equation for converting matter into energy), to replace space and time with a new entity of a space-time continuum which can be deformed. Afterwards, de Broglie proved that in nature, there is no such thing as particles or waves, that it's all wavicles. Universal duality.

As with Lupasco, the tertiary is included, not excluded. The model I was working on had space-time geometry itself being dual. Space-time was concurrently continuous-discontinuous, concurrently reversible-irreversible, regardless of level. I remembered the bracelet of the woman on the bus, the one with the snake swallowing its tail. A cyclical space-time that generates itself and destroys itself. How can all the levels of the world be connected? Geometrically speaking, the ouroboros snake resembles a Klein bottle. If the future and the past influence each other, as Wheeler surmised, then maybe space-time has the structure of Klein's compact space, where the small infinity and the large infinity touch each other, thus overcoming the barrier of Planck's time. There, beyond the most rapid moment, close to absolute stillness, lies the *whole* history of the world, and below Planck's length, the shortest length in the universe is not the void, but, paradoxically, the *entire* universe.

Words order one after the other. We think reality is the same: nicely ordered seconds, following one another in single file. When in fact, everything happens simultaneously, instantaneously. Movement, stillness, illusions both of them, created by the bottleneck in the hourglass of your mind. Time. Your mind is the bottleneck, *capisci*? Your mind is the camera. Click, click. Your mind is the unique stage on which this unique play is being produced. Reality as a show. Scene after scene after scene. Wake up, man! Stand up and leave this airless room! Break this mechanical toy, this infernal automaton that orders your life in waltzing time, one two three, one two three. Destroy the grinder that transforms every one of your moments into mincemeat.

I looked outside. The snow had stopped, and at approximately sixty feet from the hotel I could see the wide black belt of the river. Time. Time isn't a river. Heraclites was wrong.

Even less a frozen river. Parmenides was wrong too. Time is a bomb. How to defuse it is the only question.

I fell asleep instantly.

The next day I was woken up by the phone. The receptionist told me there was someone waiting for me in the lobby. I remembered the car I had booked. I looked at my watch. It was a quarter past eight. I was late.

The bearded guy from the rental car agency handed over the keys without asking me anything. My company had already paid for everything. My car was brand new. I signed some papers. I had to return the car on Monday morning. We shook hands. Without a word, he put on his gloves and left.

I went back to my room to have a shower. Outside it was snowing solemnly above the river. While shaving, I winked at myself in the mirror. I paid for the hotel and started whistling once I was in the car. I had breakfast at a creperie, "Au petit coin Breton." Strawberry jam and chocolate sauce. A dash of rum. Small pleasures, simple pleasures. If you don't make waves, if you keep a low profile, you might end up having a few quiet moments, if you're lucky. I got in the car and set off for the sugar hut.

Everything around me was white. I cracked open the window—the cold air cut in like the blade of a knife. The road had been covered in salt. Canadian road maintenance crews are extremely efficient in the snow. The hut was a hundred miles north of Quebec City. At least an hour and a half through snowdrift and frozen forests. I switched on the radio. The road followed the St. Laurent River right up to where it flowed into the ocean. It was straight as a rod, following all the hills on the coastline without a single curve. Sometimes the slope was a bit steep, and when the roads froze over, it was slippery.

My former students at Stanford would have died of laughter if they could have seen me now. In winter, the sucrose-rich sap accumulates in the roots. When spring starts, the sap starts rising into the trunk of the maple and up to the branches, giving them the nutrients they need to grow. It's important to have great variations in temperature for the sap to rise. On cold nights, with temperatures in the minus figures, the sap is attracted to the top of the tree. During the day, when the thermometer rises above freezing point, it goes down again, thanks to gravity. Indians and the first settlers would splice open the maple tree with their tomahawks and axes and let the syrup flow into little wooden buckets hung around the tree. Nowadays they use systems of plastic taps fastened to the tree and colored plastic tubing. The network of plastic tubes between the trees is then brought into an intermediate pumping station, and then the liquid is transported to the sugar house.

It was snowing more steadily now, the skies hung low over the earth like a gray blanket. I switched on the radio. News, adverts, meaningless discussion. Sweet Quebecois language. I yawned. Finally, I managed to find a music station.

Maple syrup extraction continues in a series of machines which use reverse osmosis to remove water from sap. The syrup is then boiled for hours in a huge cauldron of stainless steel until it reaches a certain standard density. It takes approximately 40 litres of sap to obtain a litre of syrup. Steam is released through special chimneys directly above the cauldrons, and if you go near the huts you can tell at once by the smell if the evaporator is working. Some find the sweet smell quite tempting. I think it's sickly. Sometimes, before meeting the suppliers at their sugar house, I need to wipe off the expression of disgust from my face. The receptors for the sweet taste are on the tip of your tongue, and experts will put just a few drops on the tip of their tongues to appreciate the freshness of the syrup, before dipping their whole tongue in it to tell you instantly if it's too smoky, too salty or too bitter. The better the quality, the lighter its color and taste. The sugar content is calculated with the help of a refractometer and is measured in Brix levels.

The refractometer is a small handheld machine with a little hole in which you put a drop of the syrup, and the electronic display shows you the sugar content in percentages. I also had a glucometer and a Lovibond colorimeter with me. Those endless hours spent in a lab in the first few years at university proved worthwhile, after all.

My job consisted of paying visits to the maple syrup farms, measuring the quality of the syrup and then creating a system of classification that my colleagues in the commercial department could use to negotiate wholesale purchases.

The sugar house I was visiting now was rather far removed from the commercial routes of the company I was working for, but it had had good reviews in the previous years and, thanks to the quality of its syrup, was now one of our main suppliers.

Beep, beep, beep. An audio signal warning me that the Panini network had stopped calculating. Just then, to top it all, my mobile went off. I stretched out my right arm and opened the laptop. Black and white shadows I could not understand. The mobile continued ringing but I couldn't remember where I'd put it. I turned toward the back seat. Where was it? On the radio, a chap with a slightly hoarse but caressing voice was singing. I can't remember the name of the singer, but the song was called "Il ritorno di Giuseppe." His voice, clearly enunciating every word, was very familiar; I involuntarily smiled.

Stelle, già dal tramonto,
si contendono il cielo a frotte,
luci meticolose
nell'insegnarti la notte.

A dull thud and the radio stopped. The light had changed suddenly, as if night had fallen and the whole sky was lit up in neon lights. I felt a salty taste in my mouth, and on my forehead I felt something sticky like maple syrup. I looked to my left, out the window. It was snowing with huge flakes, like tropical butterflies. White over white, white next to white, white through white, white, white, here, white, white there, white everywhere. The snow had a supernatural glow as if it had been dreamt up by somebody who had forgotten its details when trying to remember it. As if it had been painted by a blind man who had never seen snow. Suddenly the radio came back on again.

E a te, che cercavi il motivo…

I put my hand up to my forehead. How much time had passed? What was happening? Beep, beep, beep. Where was that sound coming from?

On the side of the road, I saw a human shape. At first, I thought it was a snowman, but when I looked closely, I realised it was a man dressed in a white snow jacket who was signalling to me. He came towards the car and asked me in broken Quebecois where I was going. The first thing I noticed was that he wasn't wearing gloves, in spite of the cold. He had a broad, olive face with wide-set, narrow eyes. His black hair was fastened into a pony-tail. I replied that I was going to a sugar house. He asked me if I would mind if he came along too. I invited him in. I restarted the engine and switched on the radio again. One station had adverts for car tires, another was going on about a law that had just been passed through Parliament. I couldn't find any music station.

Unexpectedly, the man started speaking very rapidly: "Dead people feasting on cadavers. Dead word, dead images, dead sounds. They surround themselves with other dead people and dead objects. Dead attracted to dead. The soul of the white man is like an abandoned house. Money, money, more money. The flutter of it spreads the smell of rot throughout. Tauviqjuak, do you know what that means? The great darkness. Here in the north, it only lasts a few months, but in your souls, the great darkness is forever."

The man had rattled all of this off in machine-gun fashion. I have to admit I was a bit scared. Maybe it was a madman who had escaped from an asylum. I switched off the radio.

"Who are you?" I asked.

Instead of answering, the man whistled. "Oanga. Oanga. I am who I am. You want to know my name? For you my name doesn't mean anything, I could be called who-knows-what. But I won't lie to you, my name is Ukpiq Quularuq. In Northern Inuit language, quularuq means rumbling stomach, and ukpiq means owl. So the whole village made fun of my name. Especially an old grumpy man called Ugjuk who liked to needle me. Quularuq Isumalluabiitchuq. In other words, 'Stupid Tummy Rumble' or 'Ukpiq Papik,' 'owl tail.' I wouldn't answer and then he would continue 'Ixiappak Igitak,' which in our language means poor orphan. Then I would really lose it and shout: 'Ugjuk utchuk, maguruk, uqsruqsfnitcuq quluularuq,' in other words, Ugjuk is a barking cunt who smells of seal oil and who rumbles.

"Ugjuk seemed to go mad when he heard that and would cry out 'Quularuq Isumalluabiitchuq Uqaalaruq,' which means 'Stupid tummy rumble is saying stupid things!' In winter Ugjuk would chase me around his igloo, in summer around the animal-hide tent in which I lived with my grandma. To calm him down, grandma would start shouting at him too. Ugjuk would chase after me, my grandma after him. Then suddenly grandma would stop and laugh and say that it was our fate to run around in circles like foxes and hares. 'Ugjuk nakuupiabataqtuq,' my grandma would say, trying to create some peace, 'Ugjuk is very good.'"

"So you are Inuit?"

"Inuk. Inuit is the plural. It means people. I am inuk, so a person."

We both fell silent. The road was completely covered in snow. I couldn't see anything in front of me because of the snowfall. I couldn't even tell if we were moving or not.

"How did you get here?"

"It's a long story. Maybe I'll tell you some day. Do you like stories?"

"I don't know. Depends on the story."

"I am a storyteller. I travel from here to there and bring people stories. I will tell you a few stories and if you like them, you can give me two dollars for each. Whaddya think?"

"Tell me one as an example first. Your stories make the journey go faster. After that, we'll see."

Ukpiq sighed deeply.

"I know this story from my gran. She would tell it to me sometimes when I went to bed. Every time the story was a little bit different. Gran didn't have a great memory and so she had to invent new versions of it each time. In a village there was once a troll. As soon as someone died and became a ghost, the troll would gobble them up. After eating so many ghosts, the troll got fat. The whole village was terrified of this insatiable troll.

"One day a man in the village loses his wife. He loved her very much and was very sad when she died, so his wife returned as a ghost to comfort him. But one day, she did not appear, and the man realised that the troll must have eaten her. That night he anointed himself with seal fat, covered himself in broken white shells and went outside in the dark. As soon as he saw him, the troll jumped up to eat him. The man ran to the river and jumped onto the other side. The troll, being very fat, couldn't jump of course. 'How come you are so agile?' the troll asked. 'If you tell me your secret, I promise not to eat you.' 'I drank rainwater,' the man said. The troll, who was also a powerful shaman, ordered rain to fall and swallowed as much water as in a small lake. The rain washed away the shells from the man's body, however, and when the troll realized he had been tricked, he swallowed the man whole. In the humid depths of the troll's tummy, the man was about to drown. Suddenly, he heard a voice, 'Take this harpoon and tickle him under his bellybutton.' He recognised his wise wife's voice, so he grabbed the harpoon and tickled the troll as advised. The troll burst into such uncontrollable laughter that his tummy burst open like a chestnut on the fire. And that's how fog came onto the earth. Did you like my story?"

"Cute. Now I know why fog smells fishy. Do you Inuits believe in ghosts?"

"When someone dies, we wrap them up in caribou skin and bury them in the ice. Old people are buried with their feet facing west and the children with the feet facing east. Young people are buried with their feet facing south. After death, the spirits go to Adlivun, the shadow realm under the earth and the ocean. Their souls are purified there before setting off on the great journey to Quidlivun. The Moon Realm. They might have to wait for more than a year, so they get bored and come back to earth as ghosts. What do you do?"

"I work as a technician at a company that sells maple syrup. However, my real passion is physics. I try to understand how the world we live in works, the universe, the planets, the sun, the stars."

"Well in that case, let me tell you another story." He rushed into it before I could stop him. "The Moon and the Sun were brother and sister. The Moon secretly fell in love with his sister, but he was ashamed to reveal his true feelings. One night, Moon covered his face with ash, so that the Sun would not recognise him, gave her some blackberry wine to drink and made love to her all night long. In the morning, it started raining and there was a hole in the roof, so the drops fell on Moon's face and revealed his trickery. The Sun knew at once who he was and furiously leapt up from the bearskin and shouted: 'You are never again going to touch me!' It was very cold. She left the house wrapped in bearskins and started running away. The Moon woke up too and went outside naked, running after his sister. Running through the forest, their long dark hair got entangled in the branches, heavy with moss and fireflies. The hair that got caught on the branches gave birth to night-time, and the fireflies became stars. Since that time, the Moon shivers with cold and runs after the Sun, who is sweating in her white polar bear skin."

"I see you Inuits have an explanation for everything. But how did the wind appear, Ukpiq?"

"Let me tell you how the wind came about. Ulluq was a very clumsy hunter. Everything he touched went badly wrong. One day, while he was preparing an arrow, he accidentally swallowed the tip. His mother gave him some reindeer milk to help him get rid of the arrow tip. But that day, Ulluq was going to hunt for whales. While hunting, he farted so powerfully that the arrowhead came out and hit a young whale in the left eye, killing him on the spot. The mother whale was so mad, she started burping and the whole ocean was billowing. That's how the wind started."

I had to laugh. "Ukpiq, I heard that you Inuits have ten different words for snow. Is that true?"

"Every snow is different. There is white snow and black snow, sweet, bitter and salty snow, bumpy and smooth snow, snow mixed with grass, snow melted by the rain, cold snow, lukewarm snow and snow that burns you more than fire, snow that shivers in the wind, snow like dragonfly wings, snow settling softly like a dream. There are mountains, hills, castles, turrets, eyes and ears of snow, snow bears, snow reindeers, snow whales, snowmen. My name Ukpiq Quularuq also means snow. And I am sure your name, even if you don't know it, means that too."

"So you think everything is snow, Ukpiq."

"Everything is snowfall, yes, except for a croaking crow, who was punished for trying to swallow the sun. He alone cannot be snow anymore."

"Ukpiq, who told you all these stories?"

"Till I was ten, I saw the world through a caribou gut. My gran told me that when I was born a meteor struck earth, or as she called it *Ulluriaq Anaappuq*, a star shat. This was such a powerful sign, that my mother didn't dare to look at me for two years. So, my gran raised me. Then my mother fell ill and went to the moon. My gran told me the only difference was that the people there go about upside down, the leaves are blue and the reindeer only eat grass on the left-hand side. *Puikkaqtuq*, mirror images. Sometimes when I went fishing with my father in spring, I would see icebergs in the sky. Gran said that's what life is like on the moon.

"Mother had cramps and couldn't sit still, it was so painful. One evening she came out of the igloo and crouched down with her head in her hands. The wind was blowing like mad, ready to blow out the stars, which were sparkling like hungry wolves' eyes. Mother covered her head with a caribou hood and heard suddenly 'Woah Tirie'tiang, woah Tirie'tiang!' It was Taqqik, the man on the moon, who had heard Mother's moaning and had descended from the skies in his sledge, pulled by the red dog, Tirie'tiang. Tirie'tiang was taller than ten igloos. A single push from his paw could roll the moon about like a ball. Taqqik invited my mother into the sledge with him and told her to close her eyes during the journey. Her stomach cramps disappeared as if by magic. She got into the sledge, and it started gliding on the snow with a slight groan. After a while, my mother felt how the sledge was tilting and the cold wind was whipping across her cheeks. She half-opened one eye, but closed it instantly because of the tears. All heavens were coming to her and the stars were piercing her eyes like fire-tipped arrows. After a while, Taqqik told her she could open her eyes, but warned her that before she could be allowed onto the moon, she would have to fulfil several tasks that the three moon witches would give her. It was forbidden to laugh, cry or be indifferent on the moon, and the three witches would try to make her lose her self-control.

"Mother didn't even have time to be afraid. As soon as she got out of the sledge, she heard a peal of laughter, and a large ball of fat rolled next to her. Then she saw that the ball of fat had three eyes, three ears and three mouths. She couldn't see a nose anywhere, but when the smell of putrid fat reached her, she told herself that the nose must have dropped off because of that. The ball of fat started to change shape and color, and to give off a series of whistles, grunts and murmurs, turning first into a sea lion's head, then a bear's bottom, then a limp rabbit paw. Mother tried hard not to laugh, biting her lip till it bled, and she managed to pass that trial. Then when the ball of fat disappeared, she heard a clank and saw a skeleton almost entirely devoid of flesh in front of her. Only a few strips of rotting flesh still hung onto some bones. One of the eye sockets still had a green eye menacingly swirling around in it, while in the other there was a mouse squeaking hysterically. Suddenly the mouse grabbed the eye and ran away with it in its mouth. The skeleton's jawbone started to click mournfully, 'Nuna Abnalauttaaq, Ikayutlavifaa?' Or 'Earthwoman, can you help me?' My mother felt sorry and stepped on the tail of the mouse, who dropped the eye. She picked it up and gave it back to the skeleton, who thanked her.

"Taqqik said: 'Enough for today. You have successfully passed your second test. Come inside.' The man on the moon asked my mother to be his wife and she accepted without hesitation. Shortly thereafter, she got pregnant. One day, while Taqqik was away hunting, she was visited by an old woman. She had red eyes and white hair right down to her ankles. 'How come it's so dirty in here? Earthwoman, do you never clean up?' My mother then lifted up the caribou hides and found a crack under one of them. Without suspecting a thing, she looked through the crack and saw the earth and my gran salting fish and me playing with a dog near the tent, and she remembered us and started to weep. The third witch (for it was her) then told my mother she had to leave the moon at once. When Takkiq came back and heard what had happened, he frowned and, without a word, sat my mother on the sledge and sent her back to earth. Shortly thereafter, my mother gave birth to a little girl, but I don't know how my gran knew all this, because I never saw my mother again.

"My gran says that the sky is a very high igloo and the stars are the holes in the roof and if you go as far up as you can and look through them, you will see the roof of yet another igloo, even higher, in which you can see other stars through which you can look even higher, and so on forever. One day, my father set off fishing and he never came back. I was left with my gran. The village elders said that was his *mana* and that Aipalooik took him. Every living creature—dogs, humans, seals, bears—all have their *mana*. *Mana* guides their steps. His *mana* didn't know how to bring him back to us.

"I know all of my stories from my grandma. She heard them from her grandfather, who was a shaman who was well respected by all the bears at the North Pole. I have learned from her that in winter, the sun shivers beyond the horizon and doesn't rise because it's too cold. My gran taught me all the names of the animals, *uumajuit* and *anirliit*, all that move and breathe, *nirjutiit*, the ones you can eat, *puijiit*, the ones who live in the water and come up to the surface to breathe, *pisuktiit*, the ones that roam on earth, and the names of all the birds, *niqituqtiit*, the ones that eat fish, *angunasuktiit*, birds of prey, *nunatuqtiit*, the ones that eat fruit and seeds, *ukiuliit*, the ones that stay here in winter, and all the insects and molluscs *qupiqrungit*."

Suddenly the car engine spluttered and stopped completely. When I got out of the car, I sank up to my ankles in snow. I looked around but there was a thick white fog everywhere, I could barely make out a couple of metres ahead of me. We were on flat ground covered in snow. The St. Laurent River was nowhere to be seen. The road had disappeared too. Where were we? Ukpiq got out of the car and without a word headed through the fog. I took my backpack from the back seat and ran after him.

"Wait for me!" I shouted.

Without a glance my way, Ukpiq continued marching. "Let me tell you a story. There was once a shaman who boasted in front of a bear that he could do anything. The wise bear replied, 'You can't do everything. For instance, you can't be nothing.' 'Yes, I can!' the shaman answered. 'If you don't believe me, eat me.' The bear ate him slowly, bit by bit, first one ear, then one arm, until he devoured him completely. An old seal hunter told me this story, and he said that the shaman won in the end. But I think it's the bear who won. What do you think?"

We had reached an oval building with soft, cartilaginous walls. To go in, we had to pass through a narrow, dark entrance.

"We've reached the sugar hut," said Ukpiq.

"This? This is no sugar hut. This is an ear!" I said, surprised.

"Appearances can be deceiving," Ukpiq muttered over his shoulder and went up three steps towards the tall front door.

The sugar hut-ear was full of smoke. The wooden tables were covered in white plastic cloths with a red-checked pattern. On the walls, there were dozens of pictures of bearded tourists and smiling girls.

I ordered a tea and something to eat for Ukpiq, and then went to speak with the owner. Albert was a short, plump man who panted when he spoke. He had a tiny moustache under his nose like a hummingbird. He had prepared all of the samples already. He showed me the labelled jars. I took out my refractometer and started measuring. I put a few drops onto my tongue. The quality of the syrup was outstanding. Albert puffed up with pride. When I finished, he told me: "I see you like working with equipment. And you seem to know what you are doing. I have some recording instruments too. If you like, I can show you."

"And what do you record with them? Music?"

Albert looked at me for a second and then said in a mysterious tone, "Have you ever heard of EVP?"

I shrugged. "No, what's that?"

"Electronic voice phenomena. Come and see."

Behind the ear were several round, mushroom-like bungalows half-buried in the snow. We went into the first one. It was completely empty, save for a black magnetic tape recorder and a microphone on a little table beside the window. The walls and ceiling were covered in white wool.

"For phonic insulation," Albert explained. "I got into this five years ago, when my wife died. I read in a journal about EVP and thought I might try to communicate with her in this way."

"And have you?" I asked cautiously.

"I've communicated with *someone*. Their world has very different rules from ours. I'm not quite sure if the spirit I am communicating with is my wife's. My wife is called Lucy. When I try to communicate, I come into this room and ask questions. Of course, I don't hear the answers. Then I play the tape backwards and record the sounds. I've asked the spirits many times what their names are, but they answer with all sorts of noises and bangs, and never want to tell me their names. Other questions, however, they answer most clearly. Listen to this, for example."

Albert put a tape on and pressed play. I heard some whistles that seemed to be a badly-adjusted microphone. Albert stopped the tape.

"Well, do you see now?"

I was surprised. "I heard some kind of whistles."

"*Une autre forme de vie*. Listen more closely."

I listened once more and this time, knowing what to expect, the whistles did seem to form a sound pattern. With some imagination, I could even recognise the words "*une autre forme de vie*."

"So what's he trying to say? He's an alien?"

"I don't know whose voice it is. The spirit world has its own rules. That's what I've learnt from *them*. I don't know if the spirit that said 'une autre forme de vie' is human."

"And where do these spirits live? Did they tell you?"

"Well, the cycle of existence is like a six-beat engine. The Tibetans call it *bardo* or transitional states. Three of them we can experience during our lifetime: *cheshi bardo* is our conscious everyday state, when we are awake and active; *milam bardo* is there when we are asleep; and *samten bardo* appears when we meditate. After death we all enter the *chonyi bardo*, the experience of the ultimate nature of all phenomena, which is like a profound, dreamless sleep lasting several days. Then follows the *sipa bardo*, a transitional state in which the conscience becomes active once more. This bardo is full of hallucinations and mental projections which can seem weird and terrifying. Sometimes, in this bardo, a guide appears to take your soul toward the light. Finally, the last *chenay bardo* is one of gestation, and it starts when the embryo is formed and ends when you are born into a new cycle, starting off again with the *cheshi bardo*. I believe that the sounds I'm recording belong to souls in the transitional stage, the *sipa bardo*."

"And how long does this transitional bardo last?"

"Nobody knows exactly. The Tibetans claim it's 49 days, but personally I think this waiting purgatory could last even a hundred years. Let me show you something." Albert took a book with yellowed covers from the little table. On the cover was the picture of a young woman, and under the picture was written: "*Selected Poems and Letters of Emily Dickinson*. Edited by Robert N. Linscott."

I leafed through the book in wonderment. "Nothing special, a book like any other."

Albert looked at me conspiratorially. "Emily wrote a total of 1779 poems, all without a date, and with the exception of 24 of them, all without a title." Albert turned the pages and showed me a poem under which someone had written in pencil, with a trembling hand, "April 29th, 1862." Then he turned some more pages. "Look here."

I breathed enough to learn the trick,
and now, removed from air,
I simulate the breath so well,
That one to be quite sure

The lungs are stirless, must descend
Among the cunning cells,
And touch the pantomime himself.
How cool the bellows feels!

On the side of the poem someone had written in pencil: "I am there now." It was signed "Emily." The handwriting was round and somewhat primitive. It looked like the traces left by a bird on the sand.

"Lucy was very fond of Emily Dickinson's poems, so two years after her death, I bought this book. I checked with two American experts. The handwriting is authentic. Emily Dickinson, you might remember, died at the end of the nineteenth century."

When I went back to the ear-shaped inn, I found Ukpiq surrounded by farm workers and a group of French tourists who had come to taste the maple syrup. They had also had a few glasses of red wine and they were asking him, somewhat raucously, to tell them stories about women. There were two women there with them, but neither of them seemed to mind. "More stories! Women, women!" they shouted. "We want some stories with women now!"

I noticed Ukpiq hadn't touched any alcohol.

"Yena was a beautiful girl and a shaman fell in love with her. His thoughts followed her day and night like the tides follow the full moon. The girl, however, paid him no attention. In desperation, one night, the shaman rolled over three times and turned into a small, red worm. When he got to Yena's igloo, he crept under the caribou skins that covered her and entered her vagina."

Ukpiq paused here.

"And didn't he suffocate there in the dark?" someone asked. The others guffawed.

Ukpiq continued undeterred.

"The girl's boyfriend was a very skilled hunter and he came that night to see the girl. He undressed, got under the caribou covers and started making love to Yena. It all happened so quickly that the shaman didn't have time to get out. When the scrawny penis of the hunter came into the vagina, the worm was pushed into the uterus, which shut tight like a nut. Yena was pregnant and after nine months went into labor. You should have seen her surprise when she gave birth to a baby with a beard and moustache! The hunter, certain that he had been betrayed by Yena, was furious and left. Then the baby rolled over three times and became a full-grown man once more. And since then, Yena and her shaman always lived together."

"Keep going, keep going," yelled one of the excited men. "Here's ten dollars for this story."

"There once was a woman who had teeth in her vagina. When she reached orgasm, the teeth would snap shut suddenly and cut off the unfortunate penis that had happened to venture there. The woman was very beautiful but men avoided her like a pest, so she had resigned herself, poor creature, that she was going to be alone for the rest of her life. A fisherman heard this tale and carved himself a flint condom and went to her tent, telling her that he was not afraid to make love to her. The woman got very excited, as it had been a few years since she had had a man between her legs, so she undressed immediately and asked the fisherman to come in. The fisherman put the condom on his penis and as soon as he entered her, the teeth clamped shut like a fox-trap. But when they touched the stone, they all fell apart, so the woman's vagina was now as smooth as the mouth of a baby narwhal. And so they lived happily until a ripe old age, surrounded by their children and grandchildren."

Ukpiq drank his tea slowly and, yawning, said, "That was the last one, OK, six stories are enough. I need to go to bed, it's been a long day."

Six stories, six, where have I heard this number before? *Ceva nu era deloc în regulă*. Something was definitely wrong. Six was wrong, in Romanian, a warning. "Six, six, teacher coming!" someone would say. Desks pushed back noisily, the familiar smell of paraffin wax on wooden floors. Memories of high school?

Ukpiq continued with a voice that was suddenly extremely serious. "At first, there were only men on earth and the whole world lived in darkness. There was no death back then, and men had multiplied a lot and were swarming around like ants. One of them, a brave hunter, set off to find a solution to this matter. After a long while, he found an old man carving a bit of wood on the ocean coast. The old man was taking the small wood chips and passing them through the eye of a needle made from sea lion bone. As soon as the ships touched the water, they would turn into whales and seals, while the ones that touched the earth would turn into bears and reindeer. The old man said, 'I know why you are here. Go to that mountain. There you will find a cave. Go inside and you will find what you are looking for.' The man went into the cave and saw a light. He followed it and saw a woman warming her hands by a fire. He was overcome with desire to make love to her and, at that very moment, he became mortal. From then on, all humans are born of women. And that is how light and death appeared on earth at the same time."

I heard the echo of his voice, as if he were talking somewhere very far away, inside some deep cave. I half-opened my eyes. Everything around me was white. Somewhere to my left, through my lashes, I could distinguish Ukpiq's form. I felt completely exhausted. I closed my eyes. It was far too much of an effort to keep them open.

"Ukpiq, please tell me what is going on."

Ukpiq fell silent for a few moments, then asked me, in a voice that seemed to be coming from the other end of the world: "Do you believe in God?"

"I don't know, Ukpiq, I don't know. I am a physicist and for physicists, God is just one hypothesis amongst many."

"Our Yupit brethren call him Ellam Yua, the spirit of wind and snow, the lord of the sky, earth and ocean, the soul of the world. White man has taught us to call him Agaayun. You say that Agaayun is a hypothesis for you. What use is a hypothesis when you are hungry or thirsty or about to die? But you like stories, you can't be a bad man. I'll tell you my story. It all started with Abnauraq Pixxuataqtuq. In our language, Abnauraq means young girl and Pixxuataqtuq, someone you can trust. Abnauraq was a rock-katajjaq singer, and in Montreal she changed her name to Pixi. Have you ever heard our traditional folk songs? You sing them from your throat, in a very low voice. At first you think it is a bear growling or a seal burping. I first heard her voice on radio in Iqaluit, I remember it as clearly as if it were yesterday. Grandma and I had moved to Iqaluit a few years before this, and I had bought her a battery-operated radio for her birthday. I was cleaning some fish in a yellow plastic bucket, and at first, when I heard that voice, I thought that it was the sound of the kubuyat, the aurora borealis, when it appears in the sky. I looked out the window, but the skies were perfectly clear. I listened to the song without even being aware of breathing. I thought I could detect in that voice the sound of glaciers crashing into the sea, the whistling wind, the rough waves, the bonking of the caribou, the scream of the wounded hare, the lullaby my mother used to sing to me, and my father's hoarse voice when he came back from the seal hunt. It was the most beautiful sound I had ever heard. I found all of my life in that song. When the song ended, the presenter spoke her name, Abnauraq, Pixi Abnauraq, and at that very moment I realised I was in love.

"How wonderful it is to be in love! No matter how cold outside, your heart is singing and dancing and you don't worry about a thing. I wanted to go and look for her the very next day, but I didn't have a dime. So I was, turn by turn, a whale hunter, a seal hunter, a tourist guide for those coming to Baffin Island, an igloo builder. Do you know how you can tell if an igloo is well built? You climb up on it and if it doesn't collapse under you, it's fine, you can sleep inside. Blocks cut out of several snowfalls' worth of snow can break, so you have to build your igloo with blocks of snow all from the same snowfall. I was a tuttittjuq, a snow-cutter for igloos. I learnt to read and write in Inuktitut and your language. I love books so much! Such treasures are hidden inside them! Sometimes I dream of an igloo made of books. I could lie on my back and look at their shiny covers. At night the wind would blow and all thoughts would take flight and cover the earth like dandelion fuzz.

"Five months after my gran died, I left Iqaluit. I had collected all of Abnauraq's records in the meantime and the money for the plane. I crossed the Hudson Bay with a group of Canadian geologists who took me as far as Quaqtaq. There, I was a bit unlucky. The cargo ship that goes through all coastal Eskimo villages had just gone, so I had to go round the entire Labrador Peninsula in my kayak. I passed through Kangiqsujuaq, Salluit, Ivujuvik, Akulivik, Puvirnituq, Inukjuaq, Umiujaq and at last, after three weeks, I arrived exhausted in Kuujjuaraapik. The houses in Kuujjuaraapik were built from wood brought from the south. The ground was frozen solid and you couldn't dig at all. Some houses were painted red and green, but most of them were gray, yellowish-gray. That's the first time I went into a bar, in Kuujjuaraapik. I was looking for a place to sleep, and I was attracted by the bright sign outside. After two beers, I fell asleep with my head on the table. The owner let me be, as he had just opened and needed customers. The next day I bought a ticket with Air Inuit and arrived at Dorval Airport in Montreal that evening. I wandered around town for a week, then one day I read in the papers that Abnauraq would be giving a concert at the Yellow Door, a downtown bar, on Saturday evening. I waited for her outside after the concert. It was winter, I had bought a huge bunch of roses and stuck a long, thin icicle in the midst of it. She looked nothing like her pictures, or how I had pictured her to myself. Abnauraq was small and skinny. Her long black hair was nicely combed, flowing freely down her back. She seemed very young, a child almost. When I gave her the flowers, she smiled and invited me for a drink. We walked together shoulder to shoulder along the street. I was so happy that my heart was jumping like a melting waterfall.

"At that time I spoke very little French. Abnauraq spoke your language very well, her last few albums had been recorded in French. She could only remember a few words of Inupiaq. All that evening, she told me about her lover from Toronto who had left her about three weeks ago. We found the bar we were looking for. Ile noir. Black Island. I ordered a round of vodka, then another. At some point I lost count. Abnauraq kept talking, I couldn't understand all she was saying. I followed the contours of her mouth as she spoke, the line of her neck as she leaned to one side, the playful glimmer in her eyes. I couldn't tell if I was drunk or just very happy. At some point, she took off her shoe and put her foot on my penis and started stroking it under the table. I leaned toward her and put my elbow in her armpit. 'Come on, let's go outside!' she told me. The icicle had melted amongst the flowers. We spent an endless night together. We started making love on the steps of a house, then in a park, then in the staircase of her apartment block. Excited, Abnauraq asked me to recite the names for snow in our language. Later on, she composed a song with that title, 'The Names for Snow.'

"But Tuunbaq, the evil spirit, is attracted to happiness like a shark to the smell of fresh blood. I was young and inexperienced then. What followed was sad, so I will only tell you the very end of it. Abnauraq, a druggie, was already on the road to nowhere when I met her. Regardless of how much I tried to protect her, in the end we all are born with our own *mana*. One morning I found her in the bathtub with her eyes open and a plastic syringe hanging from her forearm. I felt then that my life had finished. I felt then how pointless everything was, the chaos, the darkness of this world. I started living from day to day, begging for some coins at street corners so that I could buy myself something to drink. In the summer and autumn, I slept in the parks, but when winter came, at the first snowfall, I decided to put an end to my pain. I drank away the last bit of money I had, then set off aimlessly through town. I felt the urge to climb up high, as high as I could. I walked up a street and passed by the cemetery Notre Dame des Neiges. I got to an apartment block: Rockhill 4858. I went in and took the elevator to the top floor. I climbed up some stairs to a metal door. Forced the lock. With a few pushes, the door opened. I went out on the terrace. It was snowing with flakes as large as sparrows; the wind was blowing. Not a star in the sky.

"I half-closed my eyes to escape the wind and saw to my left the lights of the Oratoire de Saint-Joseph de Mont-Royal. I lifted up my arms and started to turn with my head thrown back. I was turning, looking at the sky that continued throwing its flakes at me, as if someone were shovelling snow over me. The flakes went into my eyes, but I continued spinning, not caring about anything. I don't know when I fell off the roof. I spun through the air like a screw. Then I suddenly stopped. Until then my life had been like a kayak on a stormy sea. Then, all of a sudden, as if someone had lit a torch, the sea calmed down.

"I was lying inside a white yurt, full of cracks and holes. Little rays of sunlight, of different sizes, pricked through the walls of the yurt as if it had been punctured by knitting needles. Specks of dust flickered. I looked carefully and the dust flecks started to form into clearer forms. The amazing thing was that I could look at all of them simultaneously, as if my gaze had expanded beyond the edges of the world and I could fit the entire universe inside it. But at the same time, the images were very detailed, as if my eyes were made up of millions of tiny shiny mirrors like some cosmic dragonfly.

"When you're out hunting a whale, at some point, when you've exhausted the creature, she will go underwater and then surge up unexpectedly, so close to you, you can almost touch her. At that moment, just before the whale bursts forth, when you don't know where and when she will emerge, the seconds expand, time becomes ethereal and floats like that astronaut dressed in a white suit that I once saw on TV in a shop on St. Catherine Street in the center. I asked one of the shop assistants who that man was, and he told me he was an astronaut on a space shuttle.

"My point of view shifted continuously. I could simultaneously see the inside of a germ and into our galaxy as it looks from space. I had both the eyes of the worm about to burrow its way through a plum and those of a child about to be born. I could simultaneously feel the cold in the hand of a beggar who has just received a coin and the shredded belly of the terrorist who has just detonated a bomb. Sunset and sunrise, the fall of water, an erupting volcano, people walking on a shady street in North Africa. I could see the screens of your 49 computers which are now reflecting our tale. Your car crash, the helicopter that brought you here, my dive off the apartment block into the snow, our trip next fall in the zodiac canoe around Baffin Bay with me amusing the sailors with my stories, while you play around with the sonar trying to communicate with the whales. I could see everything. Faces, shapes, events. Everything had not only color and shape, but also sound and smell and taste, all the tactile sensations you get when you feel the contours of a stone. The sound in the eye of the storm which is the ear. I could simultaneously see every object, every face from all angles. A billion different configurations, a billion different glances. Up and down the light wave, I could see how the aurora borealis of time is generated by all these simultaneous glances, by what I chose to pay attention to, thus creating a snowfall of events all coexisting simultaneously, immovable till eternity.

"I don't know how long my fall lasted, a second, a century, a thousand years. Then there I was, in the snow, up to my neck in a snow drift. How much time passed? I cannot figure it out. For a few moments, time had moved in a different direction, maybe perpendicular, straight up, like a mast in a frozen ocean. My bones ached. *I'noGotied*, do you see this pouch? It's a talisman my grandmother gave me and I take it with me wherever I go. It's covered in seal skin and inside, it's full of lard. That night, *I'noGotied* protected me. That night I discovered all my suffering was futile. Man cannot know Agaayun's thoughts."

The screens of the 49 computers light up intensely, throwing colored shadows onto the walls of the loft. If you look at them carefully, you can distinguish us, lying there in our white beds, with our wrists tied to the metal bars, so that we don't pull out our drips while we sleep. Suddenly the light goes off and all the screens melt like ice cubes and turn into 49 blind whale spouts.

All the people here are dreaming, connected to their machines, which breathe for them, sinking into a white abyss from which dreams emerge like icebergs. The ICU is built in a circle around the nurses' station where they monitor cardiac rhythms, EKG routes, in monotonous repetitiveness, until every now and then a blip appears and the machine beeps and a thin roll of paper records the glitch like a telex machine. A nurse tears it off and sticks it into a folder with dog-eared black covers.

"Bip bip bip." The staccato note of a pager. A hurried voice announcing a new intake. A nurse in a pale-pink uniform approaches with a syringe in her hands. Around her neck is an orange badge on which is written, in blue letters:

EMILY DICKINSON, *Infirmière*
Hôtel-Dieu, Montréal

The nurse leans over your bed and gives the injection. From your mouth, a white tube emerges, connected to a machine with yellow, red and green blinking lights. Your eyes are closed but your pupils are moving under your eyelids. You can hear me, I know you can. The fingers of your left hand are clenched around the metal bars of your bed.

I can see myself in the bed next to yours, with my head in bandages and my right leg completely immobilised in a plaster cast, emphatically reciting: "Qanuk, kanevvluk, natquik, nevluk, qanikcaq, muruaneq, qetrar, nutaryuk, qanisqineq, qengaruk, utvak, navcaq, pirta, cellallir, pirrelva." The chorus of her song. The names for snow.

Phone Call from Mars

The first few notes sound from Albinoni's *Adagio in G Minor*. It's the cellphone, a needlepoint-sized chip implanted straight into my cochlea and connected to my auditory nerve. The mirrored windows of the spherical building in front. The blue shells of the air taxis. Dusty-leafed bushes from the hanging gardens. Their average life span is… let me see, quick search… what do the statistics say? Five months and nineteen days. What do they do with them when they dry up? I don't think they burn them. Really, what *do* they do with them? I'll ask Marcel. He must know, since he votes for the Greens. Another sound signal. This time a Capriccio by Paganini. The scratchy chords always catch me off guard. I press my tongue onto the roof of my mouth and answer.

An unknown voice, yet somehow quite familiar, says my name. "Who are you?" The voice repeats my name.

"This must be a joke or a coincidence. We've got the same name."

"Please listen to me carefully. I can assure you this is no joke. I am calling you from inside yourself. If you want proof, just talk to me in your mind. I can hear you perfectly. For instance, right this second, your intestines are squeaking to remind you that it's time to go and buy that sandwich for lunch. There, it's gone now."

"Oh, yeah, sure. Very funny. You're calling from inside me. Why not from the Moon or from Mars, which are so fashionable nowadays? I can instantly prove you are an impostor. Tell me, for instance, what number am I thinking of now?"

"1307. The number on the bottom-right corner of your glasses from when you searched for the average life span of those trees, just as I called you."

"Impossible. Fascinating. Please tell me how you do this trick."

"Who are you?"

"What do you mean, who am I? Didn't you just say my name two minutes ago?"

"What does the name matter? I didn't ask you your name, I asked who you are. Tell me, have you ever been alone? Can you even be alone?"

"OK, I get it now. I've got a madman here. I'll call the police at once."

"And what are you going to tell them?"

"That a madman is calling me and spouting all sorts of nonsense."

"And what name are you going to give them?"

"Your name, of course… I mean, my name… you're right, I can't call the police. Hold on a second. Gotcha. I know. Let me check the number you're calling me from. Press the button… recently dialed numbers… That's my own number! Incredible! How do you do that?"

"Don't you remember? You reset your phone yourself yesterday, so that you could have multiple lines for calling in or out. Teleconferencing. Just what we are doing now."

"Hang on a second, you've confused me. You're saying I'm calling myself, calling me on my own phone. Is that right?"

"I don't see what you find it so unusual. Haven't you ever talked to yourself? Didn't you ask yourself then, to whom you were speaking?"

"But that's different! I'm not talking to myself. It's an unknown voice, you, speaking from outside because I can hear it on the mic of my cellphone, and for some strange reason you've got access to what is happening inside me. I am sure I heard the phone ring when you called. I wasn't dreaming. But hang on a minute, I didn't ask you the most important thing: why are you calling me?"

There was no answer. For a minute, I thought he had hung up.

"To be honest, I was getting bored. I would love to be able to speak to someone other than you, but, unfortunately, the hippocampus waves are too weak to call outside. My calls can only be received by the cell phone in your cochlea."

"Hippocampus? What does the hippocampus have to do with all this?"

"In the conversation we're having, only you are speaking in real time. Most of the phrases I am using now have been stored in the hippocampus for days, months, maybe even years. The hippocampus is part of the brain. The old anatomists gave it this ridiculous name, because they thought it resembled a seahorse. Actually, it resembles a phone receiver like the type they had in the mid-twentieth century. My answers to your questions are semi-automated, like in a hypnotic trance. Do you remember that two weeks ago you were in Zombie World and you had gotten lost in Nova Rocinha, that putrid favela in Rio?"

"Of course."

Two Sundays ago, I had been immersed in Zombie World and saw the world through the eyes of Marina, a prostitute celebrating her fifteenth birthday snorting cocaine cut with grass, dancing in some sort of a jungle trance in a Go-Go bar. The bar was full of men with naked torsos and women in bras and miniskirts, all wriggling their hips provocatively and feeling each other up like horny monkeys. There was a permeating smell of sweat, cannabis and sex.

"Do you remember when they started shooting like madmen and Marina got hit right in the back of her neck by a stray bullet and the bullet dented the telepresence earplug, so you nearly died with her? What did you feel then?"

"I panicked. I hadn't the slightest idea what to do. I could feel the sticky blood pouring down my neck. In front of me I saw a corridor of light. Then suddenly everything around me went quiet, the whole space got wider and taller and the music stopped. I had a very strange feeling, to tell you the truth. I was tempted to walk down that corridor alongside her. Then I clearly heard a voice repeating the emergency evacuation procedures, slowly and deliberately. I felt as if I were remote controlled. As if someone inside me was guiding my movements. I thought I was talking to myself, but now I realise that you were the one talking to me. Your voice. You saved me. How long have you been following me? How long have you been there?"

"Forever. It's quite frustrating to see everything and not be able to react at all."

"So who are you, really?"

"Maybe you've heard of Siamese twins, cases where one of them grows inside the other one. You can think of me as your double, your shadow self. Your twin brother. I'm your other you, or other I, if you like. The other. When we were conceived, many of my tissues were quite different from yours, but toward the end of the intrauterine period, you assimilated me fully."

"I did what? Assimilated you? Are you calling me a cannibal?"

"It's not your fault. It's nobody's fault. Siamese embryos have a life-or-death fight. In our case, your tissues developed. The hippocampus is the part of the brain responsible for memory and spatial awareness. That was the only bit of me that got fully formed. So you've got an extra hippocampus.

And that's me, your additional hippocampus, your parasite memory. That's why you can remember details that nobody else seems to notice. For most people, the present is a thin sheet of paper, while for you each second has the consistency of a stone slab on which the Mesopotamian scribes used to scratch their cuneiforms. For example, when I called you earlier, between the two rings you had time to look out the window, think about the trees, and do an Internet search. 30 milliseconds. Ask your mates how many things they can think of in 30 milliseconds. Some of my memories, of course, are different from yours, otherwise we couldn't be having this conversation. But our dreams are the same."

"So now that you've called me, are you feeling better? Happy now?"

"I can't feel anything else but what you feel. If you are happy, I'm happy. And vice versa. You can think of me as a part of you that you weren't able to access until now. You are so busy all the time. All this hopping around. All this craziness with phones, faxes, meetings, teleconferences. When you're not at work, you are on the Internet or in Zombie World. Malnourished African children, Brazilian prostitutes, Eskimos, Hottentots, chimpanzees, dolphins, condors. You are addicted to other's life experiences. Your own life is as empty as a broken drum. You've become an automaton like so many others. A little robot, a black box transmitting information here and there without any real understanding. Do you remember at all what you had for lunch yesterday? My hippocampus hasn't been corrupted yet by all this information that bombards you every single day. Part of this ancestral memory transmitted through generations is still alive, accessible, intact. If you like, I'm your first aid kit, or your last aid kit. This is just a friendly SOS signal. I'm calling you from Mars. Do you get it? That's what I am, a phone call from Mars."

"A phone call from Mars? What on earth is that? A friendly SOS? But hey buddy, what's burning? What's burning, who's sinking?"

"You and all the other people who are becoming jukeboxes. Shove a coin in and listen to the same old stupid songs. Take a good look. You are all numbskulls!"

There was a click.

That afternoon, in the air metro, I saw a mermaid. The metro was packed like a tin of hairy, dogeared sardines. Exhausted silence. Muggy. I could feel the sweat dripping down my shirt. A man and a woman were sitting together on the seats next to me, sleeping with their heads supporting each other. The woman was holding a little girl on her lap, about four years old. The girl was dressed in a checkered dress, like a chessboard. The train stopped at some station, people got off and I saw then that the girl's fingers were webbed, as if she had spades instead of hands. From the knees down, her legs were stuck together and ended in a flourish of silver-scaled fishtail. She turned her head towards me, and I saw she had mature, intelligent eyes. She stared for an endless moment, her eyes blazing intently, as dark and ferocious as two miniature black holes that absorbed light rather than emitting it. Yesterday, I might not have noticed her at all. After the nuclear bombs in the last decade or so, malformations had become commonplace... Now I too, who would have believed it... I, I, how do I know that it's me and not him talking now, which I is it? Whose thoughts are these anyway? His? Or mine? Or maybe both? Who am I referring to when I say "I"? *Hey, bro, if you're online, give me a buzz!*

Good to have a brother. Even if he's on Mars.

Dwarves on My Brain

Hyperion, a world of charms
Rises with you from space,
Ask not for wonders or phantasms
That have no name or face.
MIHAI EMINESCU

"Once upon a time." That was what they called the fashion show for the winter collection of the ElleXsir fashion house taking place against the backdrop of a story read by George Vraca, an actor from Bucharest, famous in the mid-twentieth century. It was Giovanni's idea to use a recording for the show. He was from Context Advertising. I found this out within five minutes of meeting him, as he went on and on about the psychology of advertising and the alpha waves that create a dream-like state, similar to hypnosis, and about experimenting with infrasound cannons and other such toys. Like all members of the male sex, he was trying to impress me with his genius.

Giovanni was a cute guy, with red lips, green eyes and gelled black hair, dressed in skinny jeans, a fashionably worn T-shirt and Chinese sneakers. "George Vraca was my granddad's favourite actor, and whenever I went to visit him, he would haul out his prized Grundig record-player from the closet—he was very proud of it, took care of it as if it were a jewel—and spin a record with poems read by George Vraca. The guy has a great voice, so I always thought that I would use it some day. So, for this show, I cloned his voice using a soundtrack creator and let a little robot read a story by Petre Ispirescu."

I finally managed to get rid of Giovanni, but not before he had gotten my cell phone number... which I never answer, but he'll find that out later on.

My name is Cătălina. I'm sure you know me. It's impossible not to have seen my picture in town or in some magazine. Yes, *that* Cătălina. Indeed, Cătălina. I've got a voice too, you know, the one that probably drives you mad, given the number of times you must have seen it in the TV ads. Cătălina, the golden girl, the princess Cătălina. Cătălina who travels the world in a trance. Paris, Milan, New York, LA, Tokyo. Always a new gig. My agent calls me, gives me the name of the hotel and a flight number. Now all the tickets are electronic, and all you need to do is say your name at the airport. Planes, taxis, hotel rooms. And then again, in a different order: hotel rooms, planes, taxis. Robots kissing your hand, robots taking you to the elevator, robots driving you in the limo, robots handing you perfume samples, robots packing up your shopping, robots dressing you, robots undressing you, robots speaking on the phone, robots carrying you to the bedroom, robots saying good night, robots giving you food, robots washing you, feeding you, loving you.

And then, of course, there is the Internet popping up on my cell phone. I spend most of my time on the Internet. Friends messaging me all the time, MP3s downloading from all over, blogs I surf regularly, connections, thousands of connections. In the end you get fed up with all this. It's a world as frail as a spider web. One flick and it's undone. All those bloggers who try to show you how hip and cool they are, when in fact they're as lonely as me, and if you ask them what a flower smells like, all they can do is recite the latest commercial for detergent. For about three years I had my own blog. Then I stopped it, and of course all my fans started moaning and whining about it. What a boring game, this star and fans nonsense. In the end, so as not to ruin my image, I had to let my agent deal with my website and my social media accounts, so every now and then there's a new photo uploaded there, a message like "hello, guys, how's life?" or one of my tops getting auctioned off.

No matter what time I get home, I head straight for a bath. I fill the tub and sink into the warm water like in an amniotic fluid, forgetting about everyone and everything. It's a simple recipe: a handful of bath salts, three tablets of royal jelly and then two teaspoons of acacia honey. Then, my bedtime ritual: a nettle facemask. Sleep is like a strong drug from which it's ever harder to wake up. In the morning, the circus starts: a bottle of carrot juice with apples or Kombucha, which, as you know, stimulates your digestion, and boosts your immune system and metabolism. At lunchtime it's lobster or oyster soup. In the evening, sushi with avocado, or salmon pastries, or crescent-shaped gyoza buns filled with chicken, cabbage, garlic and nira, a sort of Japanese garlic chive. Yes: the harsh diet of a model. One of my friends only ate eleven grapes per day for a month: three in the morning, four for lunch, two for supper and two for snack, until she fainted while dressing for a show. Another one went on a tomato and apple diet, had a heart attack and died of malnutrition.

The evening of the princesses and fairies show, I went to Kali to a private party. You've not heard of Kali??? How? You haven't seen the flyer? *Kali is synonymous with the best parties, perfume launches, album launches, everything that is new, stylish, trendy. This year, Kali will be the ONLY destination for real clubbing in Bucharest. Kali is the only place to be on the weekend.*

To hell with Kali! Kali is a shithole where you just keep on meeting the same people, like on a stupid merry-go-round. "Hi!" "Hi!" "How are you?" "Fine, hanging out. And you?" "Me too." "You're looking good." "Thanks, so are you." And the music is obnoxiously blaring, the loudspeakers are thumping between your ribs. The flashing lights and strobes are blinding, and your head is spinning, until you are way past caring.

The only thing those machos are thinking is about how quickly they can fuck you. It's just a culture of overinflated testosterone. They're all sure they are superdudes, supercool, superknowing, superequipped guys with their Mercs, BMWs (or boomers, as the Russians call them), their Ferraris and Maseratis. The ubercool ones now get themselves a wreck of a Moskvic or Trabant, customise it with racing car engines, and then roar up and down in front of the Peoples' Palace.

It's quite common for us to lose interest rather quickly in the male species and experiment with women. All those lonely, sad women who start dancing with each other. Ya-awn! At least with men, no matter how primitive, there is a bit of tension, an electrical current, pins and needles, something delicious and indescribable, while with women it's like drinking distilled water all day long. After a while, all that stroking and licking gets on your tits, and you want a real relationship. Something to move you, something different, something else. But when they hear that, everyone laughs at me. Dah-ling, look at you, how can you even think of such things? Then it's back to the warm bathwater, the salts, potions, rose petals, perfumed candles, all so pleasant and slow, you start almost by chance, at first just stroking your thighs and breasts. Then when you slide further down, inside, you get hotter and hotter, and your vision clouds over like a steamed-up mirror and your orgasm draws shivery-silvery spirals on it. The problem with masturbation is that it's even more frustrating than having sex with other chicks. You never get complete satisfaction; you just get more excited. Which means you become easy prey for the first idiot to cross your path.

That night at Kali, Irina told me about Hyperion.

"You've got to meet him, woman, he's the hottest thing I've ever had. I'm not kidding!" Irina, like me, is a model: blonde with a short crop, blue eyes, and everything perfectly in its place. You know what I'm saying.

"So who's this Hyperguy, the hottest ticket in town?" I was a bit tipsy already and was trying to settle my nerves to go to the toilet.

"You'll see for yourself. Here, have this ampoule. There's a red liquid in it. At night, before going to bed, when you're on your own, inject it in your vein. After five minutes, the nanodwarves will connect you to the cosmic Internet."

"Nanodwarves? Cosmic internet? What the hell is that?"

"That's my nickname for them. The dwarves are in fact some really sophisticated nanochips that connect to your nerve centers as soon as you inject the stuff, creating a kind of super-network, an interface between you and the central unit of the giant computer we call the Universe. It's totally mind-blowing, you'll see! Hyperion is a software program created by a hacker from California who disappeared about a year ago. One of his collaborators was a neighbour of mine from Drumul Taberei, who emigrated to the States, but we kept in touch. We'd meet up every time he came to Romania to see his family. We would fuck, tell stories, chill out. He's a great guy. I've known him since he was shooting spit balls at me from the balcony. He told me about this and last time we met in LA, he gave me a few ampoules."

"Are you sure it's not dangerous? What if I go berserk? How can I get rid of the dwarves in my brain?"

"It's not dangerous, honey, don't worry. Nanodwarves have been the drug of choice for computer geeks in the States for over two years now. You can go online and read their blogs. I've had two ampoules so far, and nothing bad's happened. When you want to get rid of them, all you need to do is enter a strong magnetic field and the dwarves will disconnect instantly and come out in your urine. About six months ago, I got a bit bored with them and went to the MRI center near Unirea, saying I was claustrophobic and wanted to see the equipment close up, so I got into their magnetic field and bye-bye, dwarves! But about a month ago, I got homesick for Hyperion again, so I injected a new ampoule."

"So what's the score with this superman? What's he like?"

"He's simply your dream man. Got it? Mr. Right, the soulmate you've been dreaming of all your life. The software creates the perfect model for you, according to your most intimate wishes and desires, and he can do anything your heart craves. Romantic dinner? You got it. Poetry? He'll recite it to you. The most intense orgasm ever? He'll give it to you in any position, till you're as high as the Eiffel Tower or even higher. Ah, before I forget, the connection only happens at night. It's enough to say his name while you're dreaming and he'll be there."

And then I really needed to go to the toilet. I think I was there for a while, because Irina had left by the time I got back.

When I got home, I was exhausted, but excited. So, without giving it too much thought, I went to the kitchen, took my single-use plastic syringe out, broke the ampoule and sucked up the liquid into my syringe. I patted my left forearm clean with a bit of cotton soaked in alcohol, then tied my arm tight, replaced the normal needle with a super-thin butterfly needle and injected the liquid into my veins. You wonder how I know all this? Well, my mother was a nurse. When I was a child, she used to take me with her to work, so that her buddies could see what a pretty, obedient little girl she had. She would show me all the drawers filled with medicines, tubes, cylinders in all colors, needles and syringes of all sizes, demonstrating how to make injections on a rubber doll, secretly hoping that I would become a doctor when I grew up. Well, I didn't, and now I speak to her just twice a year, for Easter and Christmas.

I then went to bed with Toni, my cuddly clown with orange hair and checked blue dungarees.

Hyperion… I can't remember at what point I said his name, which must have been like a password. That first night, I got a bird's eye view of Bucharest. I've spent so much time in traffic jams in this city, so much so that probably my innermost desire is to fly above it without stopping, jamming, screaming, swearing, loud music, wheels screeching. I had no idea how much I wanted to travel through Bucharest at a speed faster than a limping crab. That first night, he wrapped me up under his wing and we flew through the city, melting in the cool pale breeze. Bucharest looked like the background in a console game, where you run from one room to the next, shooting monsters and other creatures left and right. The edges of buildings would veer towards us menacingly, but we would avoid them at the last minute. The architecture varied from neighbourhood to neighbourhood, from the blocks of flats in the center with their roofs the color of dead fish scales, to the villas in Floreasca with round windows like portholes, then the prefabricated ten-storey blocks in Colentina, Titan, Drumul Taberei and Berceni, those maze-like ghettos in which we meandered through the dozens of cars parked end to end on the pavement, the green spaces full of dusty bushes and trees on which gangs of kids had engraved the names of boys and girls, united by obscene drawings and phone numbers. A gray city, aggressively ugly, the perfect backdrop to a horror film. This ugliness seemed to endlessly fascinate fashion photographers, who had me go to all those demolished houses and vacant plots, the most desolate parts of town. The Beauty and the Beast. The Rose of Sharon amidst the bunkers. The diva in a red dress with a cognac glass in her hand smiling at the People's Palace.

When I woke up, I was somewhat nonplussed. What had happened? Where was Hyperion? I hadn't even had a good look at him. All I could remember was a big black bird with soft wings and the blackest round eyes. Nothing else. Hyperion hadn't uttered a word and had disappeared as stealthily as he had appeared. I opened the fashion magazine on the table. *Cold, snow, humidity and variations in temperature between indoors and outdoors will dry out and irritate your skin. You will ask yourselves: how can I protect my skin in these conditions? Here are a few simple rules you need to follow every day. Before applying any foundation or powder, make sure your face is perfectly cleaned, toned and moisturised. We recommend you use the set of Allinone product set which contains everything you need to cleanse and moisturise in a single handy packet.* I closed the magazine with a yawn.

The second night, I was swimming in the ocean. He had taken on the form of a dolphin with blue-gray skin, dashing through the water, squeaking and grinning at me with rows of big shiny teeth. He would dart and jump out of the water, with huge splashes, then dive back into that unbelievable underwater world of extravagant shapes and colors. I was swimming very close to the surface; sunlight reached us in delicate iridescent tremors, as if we were lying at the bottom of a swimming pool and watching a parade of tropical fish going by. The turquoise parrot fish with yellow stripes, the angel fish with her delicate profile that nevertheless somewhat scarily resembled Darth Vader, the trumpet-fish, skinny as a supermodel, showing off fish fashions, languorous moray and scorpion-fish like a jagged edge of concrete, yellow box fish with black dots, like some Pointillist painting by Seurat, and then hundreds of little red seahorses arching their tails into a clockwork coil. And then butterfly fish with their tiny spotted fins and black-and-white pyjama-clad bodies, the toadfish all puffed up and grumpy, as well as orange coral and sea anemones, with their blue tentacles, green shoals of goatfish and sleepy pufferfish floating like astronauts in space stations at zero gravity.

Hyperion did not say a word this time either. This fish dream reminded me of a show I had last spring in the Monaco Aquarium, with the paparazzi flashes clicking like castanets among the basins filled with tropical fish.

The third night, I found myself in a garden set in a valley between two hills. The setting sun bathed the entire valley in a dense light the color of pomegranate juice, while he appeared amongst the olives and rhododendrons in the shape of a white unicorn with curly hair like a merino sheep and black eyes framed by long, curled eyelashes. The garden was a symphony

of aromas and shades of Mediterranean plants, first the over-
ture of wild mint and sage, then the delicate violins of nard,
the oboe-like trills of aloe vera and sweet calamus, the French
horn of myrrh, the piano tones of gum cistus, the cello solo of
lavender. That dense honeyed light, all those fragrances inter-
mingled, his eyes so tender and sad, those flowers rising up
in the air and waltzing around us in a circle of fantastic swirling auras, my memories of my grandmother and her country
garden, all those aromas that I had locked up with seven seals
at the very back of my memory chest were still as intense,
alive and beautiful after twenty years as they had ever been. I
started to cry quietly. For the first time, then, he spoke, "Why
are you crying? Please don't cry! When you cry, the whole
universe is suffering."

I woke up in my bed, my pillow drenched in tears. On the
night-table there was a white camellia in front of the mirror. I
tried to smell it, but it had no perfume. I looked in the mirror
and said clearly, emphatically, "Hyperion."

Instantly, I saw the curtain moving; through the half-
opened window a cold current of air blasted into the room. I
shivered. I turned my head to glance in the mirror and then,
for the first time, he appeared in human form. He was tall and
slender, his black hair slicked back, high cheekbones and black
eyes that sparkled with almost unreal intensity. He seemed
very young, almost adolescent. He was sad, a little haggard,
and his sadness was contagious. I felt an irrepressible desire to
hold him in my arms, but when I turned round again, I realised
that there was no one behind me, that, in fact, he only existed
in the mirror. Was I dreaming? Then he spoke again.

"Cătălina, the world I live in has rules that are entirely
different from yours. In my world there is no birth or death, no

hatred or love. I don't know what it means to love or to suffer. In all my eons of existence I have never done those things, but yesterday, when I saw you crying, something new, unbelievable, happened to me. I fell in love with you, Cătălina. Come to my world, let us fly together amidst stars and galaxies, let us wander through the universe like two eternal rays of light. Leave behind this vale of sorrow, leave behind your useless rag of a body and come!"

He had almost convinced me, but then he had to mention this body and useless rag thing, and the magic just dissolved, so I answered curtly and succinctly: "You think you're something special, but you're just like all the others. You want me to give up everything, while you don't give a thing. On the one hand, you are attracted to me, pay me compliments, say the whole universe suffers when I cry, blah, blah, but on the other hand you tell me to leave my body behind, this body that for better or worse earns me my keep, my decent, honest keep. No, I won't follow you, but, if you love me as much as you say, then why don't you descend into our vale of sorrow? Come to earth, Hyperion. Not like some ghost barely discernible in night-time mirrors, but like a man of flesh and bone. Hyperion, I am a woman, do you know what that means? I want to be touched, caressed, kissed, I want you to come next to me, feel you inside me, Hyperion, I need to embrace you, come to me if you love me!"

His shadow trembled in the mirror and, for a second, I thought he would disappear. He looked me in the eyes for a long time, then whispered: "I'll be there, wait for me, your wish is my command." I don't know what happened afterwards, because my eyelids were drooping, I put my head on the pillow and fell into a deep, dreamless sleep.

"Yeah, man, like I told you, all I'm getting from her is push-back. She keeps on saying no, and if you insist, if you barge in, then she sulks," said Giovanni.

Giovanni's conversation partner was a tall, plump guy dressed in a black leather jacket with "Hell's Angels" written on the back in puffed-up red letters, black jeans, and high black biker boots. He would nervously throw back his hair every now and then, readjust his sunglasses with his left hand, trying to give some order to his long rasta locks. The two young men were seated at a wooden table on the actors' terrace just behind the Intercontinental, in the shade of a green parasol, with two-pint glasses in front of them. Their blue biker helmets sat on the table in front of them.

"So, tell me, what happened?" asked the biker.

"Well, since you've seen her pictures on TV and so on, I don't need to describe her. But in real life she is even more of a hot tottie! Lips, tits, all a perfect ten, man! No silicone enhancements or anything, just all there by nature, straight from her Ma! That girl really feels you, she feels, understands, no need to explain things to her, shove the instruction manual at her. Sex with her is like a jazz concert, each one improvising with the other tune. Three months ago, I'd tried to get a date with her, but she tricked me, gave me the wrong cell number. But I was smart. I got the real number from a friend of hers, Irina, who, now that I mention her, is a first-class hooker. She can give a blow-job like no other, make you rocket into space, even the deep-throat tramp would be envious. But let me get back to my Bella Belladona story. So, I send her a text, 'what you doin' tonight?' and she answers, 'How did you get my number?'. I just brush past that, saying 'tell you when I see you. Let's meet at a concert in Karma.' She swallows the bait and we meet in Karma. I order a bottle of champagne, get my buddies there to bring it to us in a private room. After two glasses, the babe loses her hairpins, lets her hair down and I lost it, man. Like her hair shut down the light in my head. I lean forward across the table, kiss her slow and hard on her lips. She closes her eyes, so I'm guessing she likes it, and I thrust my tongue into her mouth and put my hands on her butt, push the table so it blocks the door, and, without further ado, take her panties off and bang her then and there, nice and easy. In and out, rocking and rolling, Cătălina moaning and sighing, and I'm banging it out like the elves in Santa's workshop. The guys in Karma are all friends of mine, know what's up. I did that advert with them with the bison, so the guys pretend not to see a thing, and it wasn't the first time I'd fool around with someone in the private room. Meanwhile, my woolly sheep must have been drunk, because while I was busily pumping her, bent over the workbench, she wasn't saying anything like 'yes, yes' or 'give it to me' or 'oh, my God,' all the things that chicks usually say when you give it to them good. She was just muttering 'forgive me, forgive me' and then, when it was over, she cried till her mascara ran down her cheeks and whispered a single word, which left me speechless: 'Hyperion!'"

"Weird, man! What did you say?" The biker was staring at him, his glass still halfway between table and mouth.

Giovanni sighed: "What could I say, I pretended not to notice, didn't say a word, didn't want to spoil her pleasure. Chicks have all sorts of funny stuff going on in their heads. It's best not to look too closely..."

The universe all emanated from a single dot. Where is that dot now, the heart within the heart, the center of all centers, MegaThor, The Demiurge, the creator of the Big Circus? Actually, questions like "where," "when," "why" and "how" are absolutely useless when it comes to Him, for there is no way you can locate Him in time and space, for he is the source of all locations and the cause of all causes.

Hyperion, however, was in love, and as we all know, lovers know no limits, so Hyperion found that which we all have been seeking: Hyperion reached that place of all places, that time of all time, beyond the absolute void, beyond absolute silence, beyond the edge of beyond and the center of the center, beyond reality and illusion. Hyperion found The Demiurge, the magician of the Beginning, who pulled the billion petals of the Universe out of His top hat. What exactly did Hyperion find, where exactly did he end up, in this journey at the speed of thought? To whom did he speak? Long after he had given up searching, Hyperion fell asleep and dreamt that he was in a vast, dark forest. The wind whispered among the branches. This whisper grew into a familiar, slightly tired voice. Hesitantly, Hyperion stepped into the forest of the voice.

"Human? You say you want to be human, have a body like all humans? A gross body, a sack of skin filled with flesh, fat, blood, marrow, bones, all reeking and rotting as soon as you die. How can immortal Hyperion crave something like that? Ageing, disease, pain, all the things you have to put up with if you have a body. Then ears, eyes, nose, tongue and skin through which you acquire all knowledge, the two members you use to move, the two you use to grasp and push, and finally, the fifth member, that tube of skin that eliminates that filthy liquid daily. Even the brain is just a collection of semi-conditioned reflexes. Instead of setting them free, it just sinks them ever deeper into the mire of material attachment."

"Yes, but humans can love. I have seen them on the street, embracing, I have seen them happy, laughing like children, I have seen their faces transfigured by an incredible light when they make love."

"For the universe to manifest itself, it needs duality. What would happen if there wasn't any tension, fight, sexes, duality? You need duality to evolve, up to a point. Hyperion, you've passed beyond that point. You can't go back. The world of humans is a dual one, while you are immortal, Hyperion, you are an evolved being made up of will, spirit, intelligence. Why do you want to go back? Think about it. Cause and effect, celestial bodies and events. The entire cosmos is simply a projection of my thought. A world as fragile as a soap bubble! If I blew just a little harder, all the stars would blow out, the planets would wander off into space like dead leaves. Humans? They pass by and disappear like haze, like smoke, like the clouds in the summer sky. Generation after generation will pass without leaving a single mark, as if they never existed. All the phenomena, all the events, all their joys and sorrow, all they feel, all they try out every day, whether they are awake or asleep, are just images from the same endless dream. Sunk in the ocean of their desires, confused by their feelings and their ideas, humans run around like headless chickens dreaming of corn feed. The walls of their minds won't let them see beyond it. Time is as far beyond them as an elephant is to the baby flea in its tail. They are afraid of time, because to them time is a slide moving in a single direction, hurling them down the inevitable chasm towards death. Humans are inferior beings, fragmented, second-hand creatures."

"Yes, but these inferior beings, these second-rate creatures, as you call them, are capable of love, poetry, illumination. At times, for a fraction of a second, humans attain a level that I have never known. Yes, it's true that human beings are incomplete, partial, chopped up, ignorant, but they contain a diamond at their center, the seed of freedom. And while I, Hyperion, was born perfect, and will finish as the slave of useless perfection, I want to become human so I can evolve, find love, be free."

"Hyperion, every level of reality has its advantages and disadvantages, there aren't any better or worse levels. You always have to pay a price, regardless of how high up you are. You've got everything, Hyperion. Why would you want to live impoverished? You who are a world unto yourself. Why would you want to bury yourself in a hole with no light? Please ask me for something else: a new constellation, a sprinkling of galaxies, a meeting of planets, anything but a miserable existence! You are, of course, free to choose. That's the first rule of the game. But before choosing, go back to earth and see what awaits you."

I waited for him for a month, two, three. Then I stopped, as I couldn't wait for him my whole life, like a fool. To get rid of this crazy story, I went to the MRI Center near Unirea and, using the same excuse of being claustrophobic as Irina did, I made my way into the room with the magnet and said bye-bye to the silly dwarves!

Or as Al Pacino says in *Scent of a Woman*: "Whenever in doubt: Fuck." Very good advice, I heartily recommend it to you too. It works. Next day, Giovanni, the guy from the

Context ads, texted me, and that night I went out with him to Karma. Perfect timing. The dork hadn't a clue what was going on. He thought I had succumbed to his ferocious male charm. When he got his hands on me and saw that I didn't object, he was as happy as a schoolboy with a big chocolate cake in front of him, sticking his chops in, gulping it all down greedily.

It's OK to reset your brain to zero from time to time. After all of that nonsense of *je t'aime, moi non plus*, after all the sticky sentimentality and pink frilly bows straight off the Harlequin covers, I needed a bit of action. On the ceiling of our private room they had attached a hexagonal mirror so that from time to time you could glimpse all the rubbing and groaning taking place. But while Giovanni was kissing me, I glanced up and thought I could see Hyperion's face in the mirror. His eyes, once so sad, now seemed to look at me with indifference, as if I didn't exist. Even though I seem like a tough chick, this really hurt me. He had given no sign of life, so I thought he no longer cared, when maybe, the truth was that he really did love me. I started crying, and then something incredible happened. I heard *his* voice saying: "I loved you, Cătălina, I loved you as no one has ever loved you before or will again. I love you and will always love you. Please don't cry, I cannot bear to see you crying. Neither of us is to blame for this. These are the rules of the game."

I opened my eyes and Hyperion was there in front of me. He held me in his arms and we made love as I have never experienced it before, love in which our earthly bodies burst into flames high in a pyre, and we melted into each other like mountain rivulets cascading over the rocks, then crashing down into a mighty waterfall, then meandering more slowly and sedately into a river that flows into the ocean, rising and falling with the tides, attracted by the rhythmic embrace of the world. The pyre extended all the way to the sky and all the waters in the ocean evaporated, so we both floated up into a field of puffy white clouds. The temperature rose further still, the whole earth became incandescent like a fireball, exploding in an array of plasma and sparks, while we continued to make love right down to the very essence of each atom, in every ray of light spread by our love-making throughout the entire galaxy, the entire universe.

I don't know how long it lasted but, at some point, I remember seeing Giovanni again in front of me, staring in bewilderment, unable to understand. A guy with his trousers down and a limp penis is pretty pathetic, so I went to the toilet, washed my face, then got a cab home.

—

I love you is a function limited in space. Nature hates voids. Since space is void, it has to be filled with something, anything.

The old man was right. Humans are born, copulate, and die, always blind, always incapable of understanding.

I went deeper, ever deeper, until darkness and light disintegrated.

—

That very night I texted Irina and asked for the email address of her friend in the States. Mihai replied at once, telling me more about the inventor of the nanodwarves. He had never met him, but they had worked on a lot of projects together. Suddenly, about a year ago, the guy disappeared without a trace, and nothing more was ever heard about him. Like Mihai, the guy was a psychonaut. His obsession was to create perfect love, something that would seriously caste any dating or sex-matching programs into the shade. A software program that would match every person on earth with his or her astral twin. Who were these psychonauts? Physicists, programmers, mathematicians, philosophers, mystics, adventurers, psychologists, and then on top of all this you add a subversive twist, a spirit of non-conformity, revolt, perpetual revolution. To call a spade a spade, these psychonauts were in fact hackers, but not nickel-and-dime hackers; no, these were hackers who had managed to crack the source code of the universe. They were hackers of reality.

I still didn't understand what was going on with Hyperion, so Mihai sent me a copy of a blog entry made by his friend. He signed all of his emails with H.

"If the world is a game, then our single goal should be to stop it, to virus its source code. But sometimes I too get caught up in this vicious circle and accept the rules of the Deity governing our universe, and to amuse myself I create these subroutines, like the nanodwarves, which are in fact the interface between humans and cosmic entities at a higher spiritual level of being. The Buddhist model of the world has a section populated by gods whose sole problem is that they can no longer evolve, so they long to regain their human form so that they can attain enlightenment and thus leave behind the circle of reincarnation. Our astral pairs are in this artificial paradise, where, even though they seem to have everything they could desire, they are profoundly unhappy. All the dual universes, whether physical, psychical or virtual, form a system of communicating vessels. The cosmic internet, the dreamworld, the World Wide Web are all parts of the same vast network that you can access depending on the speed of your brain modem, your astral body or your laptop. In all of these universes, all the events and actions are interdependent. Hyperion too, behind all of his billions of clones and subroutines, is a frustrated god, projecting our desires into a different space."

At first, Mihai told me, the psychonauts didn't realise the risks involved when trying to access the source code of reality. They forgot that this program had a far more experienced and able programmer behind it, which isn't quite fair play, but who ever said that God, or the Deity-on-call that H was referring to, was fair? It was his game, after all, and he could change the rules whenever he felt like it. Unlike the psychonauts, he could access the mainframe of the world much faster, and for him, changing the past or the future was child's play. Their naivety cost them dearly. Two of the psychonauts committed suicide within a week of each other, sticking their heads into plastic bags connected to their ovens. That was just a warning. At the same time, the market was suddenly flooded with tons of software and bizarre gadgets at ridiculously low prices, including H's nanodwarves. In the new market economy these cheap things often stem from some corporation's strategy. No one knew where these things came from, but overnight, H's blog address was deleted and all of the projects he had been working on with other psychonauts disappeared from the server. And H disappeared without a trace.

Mihai's stories got me even more confused. Who was H? Who the hell was Hyperion? What sort of game were they talking about? Who was its author? Now I really was bewildered. But I didn't worry my pretty little head about it, and got on with my life. Fashion shows, modelling shoots for advertisements, shopping, bars, private parties, red carpets, my model life in Technicolor 3D.

It's been three years since all that. In the general pande-
monium we call globalization, spirituality has become the new
rock'n'roll. Ten years ago, it was very exotic indeed to see guys
wearing bedsheets wandering around airports; now no one
pays them any attention. One hot summer day, I happened
to sit next to a guru like that on a flight to Brussels. He was
invited to an international congress on world religions. The
guru was wrapped up in a sort of cream-colored sheet, with
an orange scarf with tassels around his neck. His head was
shaven clean, and he wore dark glasses hiding his eyes. He
wore brown leather sandals. After we introduced ourselves
and exchanged some pleasantries, he told me he was as blind
as a mole and very sensitive to light, which is why he wore
those dark glasses. The guy was very charming and chatty, so,
gradually, the journey being quite a long and dull one, I found
myself telling him the whole nanodwarf story with my cosmic
lover. He meditated briefly and then tried to explain.

"Giovanni, Hyperion, H, even The Demiurge himself,
are nothing but avatars, shadows, projections of Him that
is forever nameless, him that is forever unseen. All of these
people are nothing more than stages on your journey towards
Him. It's all about portals or gates. Now that's just a figure
of speech, of course, because all of these things are within
yourself, within your inner being. Each one of them was your
gateway towards a different world, each one attracting you
in different ways: the world of humans, full of problems, but
also full of warmth and passion; the world of gods, incredi-
bly beautiful, but indifferent and cold; the world of hungry
ghosts filled with desire. But something within you carried
you above and beyond these temptations, further down the

road. What you are seeking is the gateway to freedom. And you have to find that yourself. I can't help you, other than tell you that this gateway does exist. The human mind has four distinct states: the waking state of day-to-day life, the dream state, the dreamless state, and finally the fourth state of *turya* where you will taste the sweetness of its nectar someday and then you will understand."

"But why these limited options, three gates, four states, nine heavens, why all these lists and rollcalls, these logical schemes? What if I don't want anything, you understand, nothing at all, what if none of these avatars attract me to go in any direction, simply because I find this choice annoying? Why should I choose? If I have to play a game anyway, why can't I create the rules? Why should I follow the rules set by somebody else? And you, Mr. Guru Man, aren't you bored of eating nothing but seeds and rice? Don't you ever feel the need to watch your neighbour in her bath or eat a medium rare steak with garlic?"

"Maya, my dear, it's maya that makes you speak thus. You think that dreams are simply smoke and mirrors, while your experiments in a trance-like state are real. But think a little bit about all that has happened in your life, from birth till now, and you will see that your existence is as much an illusion as any dream. As long as you cannot reach the state of pure space, where all things rest in the full essence of their being, benign and evil events will simply succeed each other like a hound chasing after a fox, then the hound turns into a rabbit, and the chase gets inverted, and so on, in an infinite circle. Your confusion comes from believing that your senses are real, when in fact everything is a dream. Maya, my dear, remember maya, everything is an illusion…"

"I was about to crack a joke about this maya business… Anyway, I forgot to mention one little detail. After that night in Karma, I got pregnant and nine months later I gave birth to Ionuț. Giovanni wouldn't recognise the child as his own, and for good reason, because the paternity test showed he wasn't the dad. Ionuț is a very cute boy. See for yourself, here's a picture. Isn't he adorable? See what intelligent black eyes he has? The spitting image of his dad, you know. Now, please excuse me, but I want to look out the window for a bit. Maybe we'll chat more later. Anyway, thanks for the explanations. Namaste and bye. Om mane padme… kerchoo!"

I sneezed noisily, turned my head and looked out the window at the gray blanket of clouds that they were flying above. Beyond them, I could see the stars flickering in the sky like fireflies.

"Dwarves on my brain," I said, smiling. "I think I'll take a nap."

The Minimalist

"...what's in front of your nose? You go into one house. There's a guy at the table. Stuffing himself. Then you go into another house. Another guy in front of the TV. Staring. Remote-controlled. Drugged. Like an insect pinned down. Another house. Another. Yet another. Your neighbours, my neighbours, from my street, my town, my century, my illusions. Not abstract beings, but horribly concrete. Little robots. Consumers."

An ocean of immobile cars. Tense, congested faces, endless honking, dust. Bucharest at rush hour, on one of the main streets, blocked by an accident, the ring roads under repair. Imagine you can view all of these cars somewhere a hundred yards above University Square. From up there the traffic-jam looks like a procession of dusty and noisy beetles, all different colors, all turned belly-side up and squeaking nervously. Then all the cars try to move at once. Stop for a beat. Then shouting, swearing. The smell of hot asphalt and gasoline. Pedestrians weaving their way between the cars. Then sudden illumination. Right here, right now. Traffic.

"All this overcrowding is because of the Gate. You see, we are a gate between the East and the West. We have always been and always will be at the crossroads where people pass. Winds, waves, migratory people, everything passes by, turn by turn, but we stay put. Just look at it."

The driver of the white Matiz who has just uttered the words above is wearing green cotton trousers and a sleeveless red top with Che Guevara's face printed on it in black. He's got a black bandanna on his head, sunglasses with huge brown circular lenses, '70s fashion, and a red bushy beard reminiscent of Sandokan, the Tiger of Malaysia. He speaks staring straight ahead, as if reading from a teleprompter while being filmed.

"You see, I've lived in the States for fifteen years. And what I've noticed is that there, people don't have limits. 'The sky's the limit' is what they say. Bigger is better. A society that is always pushing its limits. But hardly culture, civilization, spirituality. Nope, just violence, sexuality, obesity. Especially obesity. Everywhere you go, you bump into fatsos. Shameless, I tell you, shameless. You look at them and they don't give a shit about the way they look; they're not embarrassed. Round like balls of lard. Men, women, kids, just overflowing every which way with their rolls of fat, on the streets, in restaurants, in the subway. Once, in California, I was stopped at a traffic light and I could see the car in front shaking as if someone was hitting it. When I overtook it, I saw four fatties in the car, all young girls, but each one well over two-hundred pounds, listening to music turned way up, grooving along to it so much you thought the car would fall off its wheels. They were having fun, no prob! Then, after fifteen years, when they introduced compulsory GPS on all cabs, I couldn't move an inch without Uncle Sam noticing, so I didn't feel like working there anymore and came home."

"Do you regret it?" asked his passenger, sitting next to him, a man in a beige suit with a blue tie, closing his eyes and squinting in the bright sunlight.

"Not at all. Not… at… all! You always have to make choices. You can never have it all. In the States, I always felt something essential was missing. I just could never manage to have a normal relationship with people. I always felt they had other things on their mind, they wanted something else from life than me. Dollars, dollars and yet more dollars. Well, I say that about the Americans, but in fact ours ain't much better now, after the Revolution. Now all the Romanians are chasing open-mouthed after money, money, money. It's a contagious disease. And for what? What do they do with it all? Yeah, it's important to have something to eat every night, so you don't die of hunger, and to have a place to lay down your head when you come back from work, that's very true, but material things are just a starting point. They can't be the end-all and be-all of your life. You have to choose whether you live to eat or eat to live. I find it absurd to think that the universe has been trying to create someone like me for billions of years, and then I can't find anything better to do with my time than chase after money, just to stuff my face."

"So what did you do with the money you earned in the States?" asked the man with the tie in a bored voice.

"I travelled, my friend, travelled all over: Peru, Chile, Australia, China, Egypt and Israel, Malta, Italy, Greece, India, Tibet, I wanted to see the world with my own eyes, as it is, not as it appears on the Discovery channel or in travel books. I've been looking everywhere for a sign, you see."

Sweat was pouring down the faces of the drivers with non-air-conditioned cars. Some had the windows open and were smoking lazily.

"What kind of a sign?"

"I don't know, some sign: a rock, a tree, a person, a sign that life has got some meaning, that we aren't just prisoners in a slaughterhouse without exits, a sign that there is a chance, a way that we can be saved."

"And did you find what you were looking for?" the other guy asked ironically.

The immobility of the cars was absolute by now. People had given up beeping their horns, and were just leaning drowsily on their steering wheels.

"Yes and no. I've understood that it's useless to search for the exit. The way out is not to be found, you need to build it yourself, day by day. Have you seen *Fight Club*?"

"The movie?"

"Yep, the movie."

"I think I saw it a while ago at a friend's party. I was a bit tired, so I can't quite remember what it was about."

Three policemen had turned up at the intersection and were yelling something at the drivers in front.

"Well, that film had a message. The ending was a bit weird. They were scared to let all those banks and credit card companies explode so they made it out in the end that the guy was crazy. But those guys showed that nothing is impossible, that there is always a way out. You may have heard of those 15 minutes of fame that the Americans are always on about. Well, look what I've figured out. I'm a taxi driver, and in this continuous traffic jam I've got plenty of time to talk to my clients. I can use this time to have normal conversations, man to man, so I can spread the info to all those who want to know. You see, information is power, information can undermine this crusher, this shit system, this machine that turns us into mincemeat till we no longer know where we are. We need to use information to free ourselves, and do it properly, not just on paper. I talk to you, you spread the information to your friends, and so on, until slowly, gradually, first one person starts wondering, then two, then three, until in the end we all wake up and start the real revolution, not that sorry thing from '89 when all those kids died so that these bastards can now buy all their villas and companies."

The man in the suit sat up suddenly, as if he had just woken up, put his hand in his breast pocket and pulled out a roll of crumpled banknotes, thrust some of them at the driver and opened the door, saying: "I don't think we'll be moving at all today. I'll take the metro."

Half an hour later, the traffic had quieted down a little and the white Matiz had reached Romana Square. A middle-aged lady hailed the taxi: her hair was in a bun. She was dressed in a pink suit and carrying several bags.

"Drumul Taberei district, Favorit please," she said, sitting in the back.

"Good afternoon, ma'am, I see you've been shopping," said the driver, glancing in his rear-view mirror.

"Yes," said the lady, "I bought two pairs of shoes on sale at Piața Unirii and then I walked back all the way window-shopping, and found some other small things along the way. My feet are killing me and I was dreading taking the bus home, so I told myself, 'Why not a cab?'"

"Of course, ma'am, that's what we're here for, to help you. But let me tell you that you too are a victim of this grinder." Seeing the perplexed look on the lady's face, the driver smiled and continued: "Yes, ma'am, this grinder is the corporate system that tries to induce you to buy things that you don't really need. Tell me why, when you are already wearing a lovely pair of shoes, do you need two more pairs? It's the crusher, ma'am, I tell you. I've lived quite a long time in the States and

I know what I'm on about. The crusher there works beautifully. Everyone just throws their money out on all sorts of silly
gimmicks. Consumer society. And now we have it too. We
queue up to go to McDonalds and we think we're all global-
ised now. In fact, the system pushes you to consume all those
shoddy products which break almost immediately, so you have
to throw them away and buy new ones, and so it goes on. If
people stopped consuming, this machinery would go to pieces
immediately. Americans work harder than almost any other
people on earth, but they are being fooled, because they have
the shortest vacations in the world and are so tired when they
do go on vacation, they don't have time to enjoy it."

The lady did not relish the turn this conversation had taken.

"You're not a Communist, are you?" she asked sharply,
"because if you are, I'm getting out right here. My father died
in a prison in Aiud. And I notice you are wearing a T-shirt
with that Cuban friend of Castro's."

"No, ma'am, don't worry, I'm not a Communist. For Chris-
sakes, you think I'd be a Communist after all we went through
under Ceauşescu? You remember what we used to say back
then? That we were a country full of penguins, freezing to
death and clapping our flippers. In '45 the Russians killed my
granddad, beating him to death with the backs of their guns,
because he wouldn't tell them where he kept his horses. His
brother had taken the horses to the woods, to a safe place,
and my granddad held out and did not breathe a word. For a
peasant back then, horses were very precious. The Russians
stormed his garden and they probably hadn't seen an eggplant in their lives, because one of them pulled one out and bit
into it greedily, and then he coughed and spluttered, spitting
and swearing. My grandmother told me this eggplant story

hundreds of times. No, ma'am, I'm no Communist, but I'm not a capitalist either. I'm a proper certified revolutionary: I was imprisoned in December '89 in Jilava."

"OK, OK. Can I smoke in your cab?"

"Of course, ma'am, with pleasure. I don't smoke myself, but you can open the window. You can use this shell as an ashtray."

The woman smoked silently for the rest of the journey and the driver didn't say another word. When they arrived, she gave the driver a big tip and he rushed out to open her door politely.

"Thank you so much, and do come again! Here is my card."

After the lady got off, a young woman approached the cab. She was in her early twenties, wearing low-cut jeans and a short top that revealed a roaring wolf's head tattoo just below her waist. On her left cheek she had an ugly yellowish-brown bruise.

"Please take me to the airport."

"Otopeni?"

"Yes. Domestic flights." She sat down next to the driver.

"It's great to fly, if you can afford it. I heard on the radio today that on one day alone, throughout the country, there were eleven fatal accidents on the roads, with fifteen people dying. It's like Iraq here, people dying every day. So what are you doing in the countryside?"

The girl sighed. "I'm sick and tired of this city. I'm going back home to my parents. It's complicated. I've broken up with my boyfriend and I don't really want to see anyone."

"Good for you for leaving. Did he give you the black eye?"

The girl didn't reply. The roads were empty and a short while later, the car reached the Mall Plaza in Militari. In front of the Mall, a few dozen people were queuing to get their hands on the glasses, T-shirts, stickers, pens and balloons all displaying the name of a brewery.

"Just look at them," said the taxi driver with venom, "look at them all being brainwashed, hypnotised by these promotions, wandering around like sleepwalkers. There they are, waiting like children to get colored balloons and stickers. And these malls are multiplying like mushrooms. This rampant consumerism is a dangerous addiction, and we've all become a nation of addicts. We buy all the stupid stuff they feed us, and we can't seem to get enough of it. They've corrupted all of us. They've given us the illusion that happiness lies in a widescreen TV or the latest model of washing machine. We've taken all that is bad about the Americans. Crap films and Coke. Conformity."

"The Americans have long since become little robots. I know what I'm saying, 'cos I lived there. Everyone's going mad. Mad, I tell you. How many normal people do you know? We admit the violent ones in hospitals and put labels on them saying 'dangerous madman,' but they are merely the extreme cases. Those people taking the subway every day are madder by far, zoom here, zoom there, metro-work-metro-home-beer-bed. When they get home, they watch the same old crap on TV every night that keeps dumbing them down. Or take those mad soldiers who are killing people they have never met in their lives and they call that courage, patriotism, sacrifice or some such overblown bit of bombast that they have had tattooed on their foreheads. Or take those mad businessmen, stuffing themselves with money till they burst. For whom are they doing it? What use is all that fortune? But they just keep shovelling all that money in, and for what? So they can die alone, in an old people's home, with all the relatives rubbing their hands and waiting for them to die so they can inherit all their fortune? Or the crazy priests repeating words they can barely understand. Or mad scientists who wander around blind to all reality, banging their heads against so many walls that they've forgotten what they're looking for. I tell you, all mad, mad, mad, all ready to be hauled off while we keep on chewing our cud like cows at the gates of heaven." The driver stopped to draw breath.

"I've met a normal person," the girl said pensively.

"A normal person? You actually met one? Wow! Who did you meet?" asked the driver, surprised.

"I don't know his name, but this man was, honestly, perfectly normal."

"Tell me about it," said the cab driver. "I'm all ears."

The young woman leaned back in her seat and started speaking in a low voice.

"I remember one incident from my childhood, I was spending the summer holidays at my grandparents, and a stupid cat, a skinny, dirty, scruffy stray, the kind you can see in the hundreds on the streets of provincial towns, was searching in the garbage bin behind the block of apartment buildings where my grandparents lived. It was a huge metal container, painted green, tall as a grown man, and this cat was searching through it and had got its head stuck in an empty coffee jar. It was banging its head against the walls, trying to break free, like a knight whose helmet had fallen over his eyes, and the other children, my playmates, were banging with sadistic pleasure against the walls of the bin with empty bottles and sticks, scaring it half to death. I couldn't bear its muffled cries any longer. It was just about ready to suffocate in front of our eyes, so I climbed into the bin and tried to free its head. But it was really stuck: the more I pulled, the more the cat struggled in my arms like a wild beast. In fact, it scratched me so hard I started to cry, and the cat was meowing hysterically, and my hands were all cut up and bleeding. It was a real circus until I managed to get its head out, while the other kids looked on and laughed. The man I met did the same thing for me, as what I did for that poor cat. He opened my eyes."

The taxi had reached Grant Bridge by now, which was extremely jammed, with cars bumper to bumper.

"Yeah, I agree with you, we live in a world full of mad people, but somewhere there is a man who doesn't want to have anything to do with this. A man who is completely different. In this mad, mad world, as you call it, there is a normal human being. And I've met him."

The cab driver smiled, "Maybe you've met the invisible man."

"You don't have to believe me, but I have met him. This man I'm telling you about, he exists and breathes the same air we breathe. His life is so simple, so ordinary, so well adapted to his surroundings, that if you were to meet him tomorrow you wouldn't look at him twice. He speaks normally, he looks normal, he acts normal, there is nothing special about him, nothing obvious. He doesn't impress you at all.

"It was the doorman of our apartment block who first told me about him. A few months back a burglar broke into several apartments in our building, including ours. They stole a camera and some silver earrings from me, and took Vadi's music player and a laptop. They caught the thief, and the doorman came with a list of the recovered items so I could let him know the ones of ours we were missing. It was then that he mentioned the guy.

"'Funny thing,' he said. 'I've just called on the guy on the ground floor as well. You know, the one just to the left of the elevator. It's so quiet there that you almost think the apartment is empty. The cops took their gloves off with this thief, and he had confessed just about everything he'd ever done in his life. He had stolen a blanket from this guy. And since it's winter, I kind of thought everyone needs a blanket. So I ring and ask him: "A burglar broke into your apartment a few days ago."

""'Yes," he said.

""'So, what is missing?"

""'Nothing is missing."

""'Nothing at all?"

""'Not at all."

""'Look, we caught the thief and he said he had stolen a blanket from you. Look again, maybe you haven't even noticed it's missing."

""'No, sir, I assure you, nothing is missing.""

"Two weeks later, I left the faucet on in the kitchen and flooded the tenants on the ground floor. I went into this guy's apartment with the doorman to see what the damage was. I was stunned. There was nothing, nothing at all in that house. No bed, no table, nothing, nothing. Not even curtains—and he was on the ground floor, mind. Not even a toilet seat. And certainly, no blanket. The room was absolutely bare. Even a prison cell has more stuff in it than that room. Whitewashed walls, with not a thing hanging on them. Everything immaculate. Not even a fridge in the kitchen. An empty apartment, ready to be rented out.

"One afternoon, about a month ago, I met him by chance when I was leaving the apartment. He was one of those people whose age you cannot guess, you know: olive-skinned, no wrinkles. He could just as easily have been 25 or 40 years old. He was neither handsome nor ugly, of medium height, perhaps a little on the skinny side, with eyes that seemed either brown or black, depending on the light. He wore a white, long-sleeved shirt. I was intrigued by the blanket incident and approached him directly.

"'Do you belong to some kind of sect, are you a yogi or something?'

"'No.'

"'So how can you live like that, with no table, no chairs, no carpet, like a monk?'

I admitted I had visited his flat in his absence, together with the doorman.

"'Because I can live quite well without them. The rooms are small enough as it is, if you fill them up with furniture, they become even smaller.'

"'But you do realise that's not normal, don't you?'

"'Depends on what you consider normal. Actually, I feel fine the way I am, so I think I am perfectly normal.'

"'Do you have friends?'

"'I used to have a girlfriend, but she left me at some point.'

"'Didn't you try to stop her?'

"'What would have been the point? She had decided to leave.'

"'You seem completely indifferent to everything. Don't you want anything in life?'

"'Of course, I do. I wake up, listen to the birds singing outside, have a shower, eat a slice of bread with honey and leave for work. I look up and see the shape of the clouds between the buildings and I am as happy as if I were seeing them for the first time. What a lovely contrast between the blue sky and their whiteness. I breathe deeply and go the bus stop. I listen to my music on my i-pod. I live. Nothing special.' Then he excused himself and went inside the building."

"Strange," said the cab driver, "I agree with you: very strange man. What happened next?"

"Well, a nasty thing happened next. Vadi and I occasionally snort things, you know, coke, heroine, whatever we find. And Vadi can become quite violent, especially after coke or ecstasy. He sometimes would beat me up and I, like a fool, would threaten to leave him every time. But then he would give me a present, apologise nicely, and we would make up and start all over again. Until last week, when it went really sideways, and I swore I'd leave him for good. Did you see what he did to my eye, the bastard? I could have gone to the doctor and gotten him sent to jail, but to hell with that. He's down and out as it is. He sent me on Friday to get some stuff, and I was a bit drunk, as I had downed a bottle of gin with Andreea, a friend of mine who had just passed a really hard exam, and I don't know what I did with the money. Maybe I lost it somewhere along the way. Anyway, I couldn't remember a thing, and when I came back two hours later with no stuff at all, Vadi was there with three of his buddies, waiting for me, and I made the mistake of phoning him beforehand to say I'd lost the cash. He came out in front of the apartment-block and started punching me in the head. People had gathered at the windows, were staring open-mouthed, but no one dared to say a thing. And then this guy from downstairs turns up. I was crouched at the entrance and crying.

"'Please step aside so I can get in,' he said, putting his hand on Vadi's arm. But Vadi had lost it completely. 'What? You want to get beat up, too?' And he rushed to punch him. But the guy stepped aside, and Vadi's fist hit the metal post of the wrought-iron fence behind. His hand was badly injured, blood pouring out like a fountain, and he was crying like a child. He was completely high, of course. I was a bit embarrassed in front of that guy, not that he had anything to do with it. I knew I had just tumbled into this mess, so I just asked him to leave me the hell alone, that I could handle it. He didn't say anything, just went in.

"Vadi went upstairs after that to put a bandage on his hand and told his friends, who were so out of it they wouldn't have even been able to tell you their names if you asked. He wanted them to deal with the guy who had broken his hand. Oh, sure, he could have handled him with just one arm, of course he could have, but his buddies supposedly had to hold him down, so he wouldn't kill the guy. He claimed he was so mad that who knows what he would have done.

"Which was nonsense, just Vadi's stupid bragging. He was a coward, all mouth and no balls. He just wanted to show off in front of me. While all this was going on, they decided to go into the guy's apartment. I called the police on my cell phone.

"When I went into the apartment, all four of them had gone completely bonkers. They were saying all sorts of weird things that made no sense at all. They muttered something about sounds and lights. They were spinning around in that white, empty apartment trying to find something to grab, to destroy, to break, but there was nothing there, and they were trembling with fury like dogs with rabies. Vadi said he couldn't see, and was banging his head against the walls. When the police arrived, he was delirious and kept asking where Bârlad was, because he needed to go to Bârlad. The second guy said he could hear voices telling him repeatedly: 'You're missing an ear. You've got two now, but you had three before. Where's the third one?'

"The third guy was itchy and kept scratching himself. He had taken off his shirt and scratched his back so much that blood had started coming out. The fourth one was crawling on the floor and said that if he stood up, the room started spinning."

"And where was the guy?" asked the driver.

"He came back into his apartment at the same time as the regular cop, who had come with two armed policemen. He claimed that he had popped out to the store to get some mineral water and didn't know a thing. He looked at the four men and, to my amazement, a miracle happened before my very eyes. That's what I have to call it: a miracle. All four of them, who had been acting like madmen who had escaped from Bedlam, all those macho men full of airs and graces, suddenly, beneath his calm and bright gaze, began to whine like cry-babies and beg his pardon for entering his house uninvited. The policeman asked if he wanted to file a complaint for breaking and entering. But he said that the door was open, so there had been no breaking. Why should he file a complaint, they were his neighbours, after all. Something broke inside me at that point, and I realised I could no longer go on as I had. I woke up and said to myself, 'stop.' For the past week, I haven't taken any substances. It was so bad the first few days I thought I would die, but now I'm over it. So, for now, until I decide what to do with the rest of my life, I'll go home to my parents in Timisoara. In any case, I'm not going back to Vadi."

The taxi had reached the drop-off point at Otopeni airport.

"Bye then," said the woman. "Who knows? Maybe we'll meet again."

She made a quick exit, and the driver took the money without bothering to count it.

"You free?" asked someone through the half-opened window.

"Sure, come in."

All the way back to Bucharest, the driver did not utter a single word. When they reached Kiseleff, the passenger, a plump gentleman with white sideburns, a bald patch and a bit of beer belly, tried to start up a conversation, just for the sake of saying something: "The wind last night has scattered all the flowers from the trees."

"Yes," said the driver, watching him in the mirror, "we won't have much fruit in autumn this year."

The Sixth Sun

The Bible and the Apocalypse have foretold this for millennia. Moore's law even gives a rough date for it. Statisticians have calculated that very soon after an artificial intelligence program surpasses human intelligence, it will very swiftly start to create subroutines that will improve its performance exponentially, reaching extraordinary speed and calculating power until, at some point, in a flash, *something* will happen. Vernon Vinge called this moment the Singularity. The psychonauts call it the Transfiguration of the World, His Second Coming.

It was a sunny day, I'd gone out for a coffee break, when, suddenly, walking down the street, I saw the first pair of abandoned shoes. It was a black pair of shoes, woven leather, nicely positioned one next to the other, toes pointing to the main road. I looked around and saw other shoes pointing in the same direction and, next to them, a path strewn with coats and shirts, dresses, skirts, ties, trousers, socks and underwear. Not a soul on the street, just a yellow dog running ahead in the distance, tail all curled up.

I followed the trail left by the shoes and clothes. I felt at ease, light like a hot air balloon. I smiled aimlessly, started whistling a song. The heat was unbearable, so I took off my shoes and clothes and made my way through town completely naked, as if it were the most natural thing in the world. A few minutes later, however, the melting asphalt in the midday sun was burning the soles of my feet, and I regretted giving up my shoes so easily. Luckily, I found a pair of rubber-soled green flip-flops to put on. I reached a street that was going downhill, with pretty wooden houses on either side. One of the houses had a wire cage hung next to the door on the veranda, the kind you use to catch flies. The cage was nearly full of dead flies, but there were some live ones still above them. Their buzzing mingled with the buzz of the electric shock that killed them the instant they touched the wire, creating a strange kind of duet. On the steps leading up to the veranda there were several pairs of shoes, all different sizes. I bent over, picked up a woman's black shoe and hit the cage hard with the high heel. The wire mesh broke and all the flies tumbled out, scattering in a cloud of peeling housepaint through the little garden, complete with gnomes and plaster angels.

I set off once more, whistling, when, suddenly, as if my whistling had summoned an invisible spirit, the wind began to blow. I say wind, for lack of a better word to describe the hallucinatory phenomena taking place all around me. A mad wind was dissolving the contours of the buildings all around me, as if we had stumbled upon an alternative reality in which time flowed differently, staccato, like a bolero. Some strange force was shaking our world, which had all of a sudden become as unstable as a sailing boat at the mercy of the seas. Buildings vanished for fractions of a second, then reappeared with crooked lines, as if drawn by a child. An impulsive, moody wind, blind and deaf, a mad wind, product of a crazed mind that can only feel vertigo.

Buffeted about, pushed forwards and backwards by unruly gusts of wind, I found myself in front of the Olympic Skating Rink. There were a few thousand people gathered there, all naked, all gesticulating and shoving as if they had been drugged with laughing gas. I joined the crowds and entered the building. It was so cool inside, I got goose bumps. And there it was, the magnet that had attracted all of us, the source of those mental pheromones that had us wandering through town like sleepwalkers: a tall black column, emitting deep sounds, like some dull humming. The column was in the middle of the ice rink, covered by hundreds of diamond-shaped tiles, all connected through a complicated circuitry of golden wires, which gave it the look of a mysterious obelisk engraved in an unknown language.

People were dancing around the edge of the rink, holding hands and singing party songs, as if they were in a trance. A few black mongrels were barking and darting amongst their legs, as well as a couple of scruffy cats caterwauling hysterically. In the generalised chaos there, people started hugging and kissing each other at random. I hardly know how I found myself with a plump girl in my arms, smelling of lavender, with moist, warm lips. All around us, couples and groups were forming in every conceivable position, like in an intricate end-of-world orgy, yet we continued to kiss slowly and delicately like teenagers. The ice rink was replete with sighs, groans and obscene remarks, interrupted every now and then by a round of barking and yowling.

Then there was a sharp whistling sound and, to our surprise, the walls and roof of the skating rink dissolved like clouds passing in front of the sun. I turned my head and noticed that all the buildings around the rink had disappeared. In their place, there were now tens of identical columns. A multitude of solar panels appeared on the column, like green fish-scales, and then, the column started to rise slowly towards the skies, like a cobra upon hearing the fakir's whistle. When it had reached the height of a skyscraper, it stopped, and above it, appearing out of thin air, a huge shiny sphere materialised, like a translucent soap bubble refracting the sunlight into hundreds of little rainbows. The sphere fragmented into thousands of colored bubbles, falling slowly towards us. White doves appeared from who-knows-where, looping around the bubbles like at an air show display.

I held out my hand, and one of the bubbles sat lightly on my palm. It was transparent, about as big as one of those baubles you find in souvenir shops, filling up with sparkly stars when you turn it over. This bubble was filled with violet smoke, curling and twisting into all shapes, pictures, landscapes. I stared at it in fascination and gradually, like on a badly-tuned radio on which you can barely make out the tune amidst so much static, memories from my childhood came to mind, things I had not thought about in years. My first interplanetary journey, the earth seen from the moon, like an orange covered in blueish-gray mould. The mole I had found in my grandma's garden one summer day, a soft, warm bundle that I had scooped up and put on the kitchen floor. When my gran touched the mole with the tip of her yellow plastic slipper, a thin whisp of blood flowed out of its mouth, and it stopped moving. A girl's laugh, happiness like a tree in full blossom in mid-winter. The first funeral I attended, aged ten. Lights and shadows. Scars and wounds. The hundreds of heartaches and lumps in your throat that make up a human life. I started crying and noticed that the people around me were sobbing silently with tear-filled eyes. As if on cue, that strange wind began to blow once more, drying up my tears instantly, lifting all the bubbles up to the sphere at the top of the column and reintegrating them.

The First Age was the Age of the Water Sun, Atonatiuh, and humans were created from ashes. They lived until a great flood came covering the entire earth, and humans became fish.

The Second Age was the Age of the Earth Sun, Ocelotonatiuh, and humans were giants. But this Sun too was destroyed. The earth was shaken to its core, and humans were devoured by jaguars.

The Third Age was the Age of the Fire Sun, Quiauhtonatiuh, and humans were eating cincocopi, an ancient form of maize. But the earth was burnt to cinders, and humans became birds.

The Fourth Age was the Age of the Wind Sun, Ehcatonatiuh. Humans were eating the kind of maize we now know, but these humans too were destroyed and turned into monkeys.

The Fifth Age was the Age of the Moving Sun, Olintonatiuh, which was born in Teotihuacan, the City of the Gods, with everything in movement, rivers and oceans, the sun and the moon, people and clouds. These humans too will be destroyed, but not before their tears have given birth to the Sixth Sun, the Binary Sun, Ometonatiuh.

Suddenly, as if someone had switched off the sound, there was silence. Words began to appear on the electronic panels of the ice rink, where the hockey match scores and the judges' marks for skating competitions were usually displayed. I glanced at my watch. It was exactly 12:01. At that precise moment, all the animals, plants, humans, creatures on Earth were receiving the same identical message, in their various plant, flesh, human languages, the same obsessive message that was flashing by like a mantra in white letters on the screens in front of us:

O, death, be afraid, for your time has come! Let us all sing now, for the empire of death has been vanquished! Come to your senses, earthlings, and rejoice! Until now your bodies were short-lived and your spirits eternal, but from today on, you will all be immortal in body and in spirit, you will never again fear for your life!

What great heavenly power lies with the Word! The Word is Him and He is the Word, and your bodies today will be Word from Word, like on the first day! Go forth and spread the good news, dance and celebrate, for from today onward, you will ditch your mortal bodies and live forever and ever, amen!

O, children of the Word of Life, spread out your wings of light and fly all over the universe, amongst all the planets and the galaxies, all the stars and the constellations, and spread through-out the Universe your laws of Eternal Love and Eternal Word, as you have witnessed them today! Love is the Universal Law that keeps the

*planets rotating and holds the suns in the skies,
love is the essence of the Universe, the secret of
secrets, the miracle of miracles! Love, love, love,
and be loved, my dears!*

The sun turned black like a bag of hair, the moon red like blood, and the stars of heaven fell unto the earth, just like a fig-tree shedding its untimely figs when blasted by a mighty wind.

In the first instance, all the atoms of organic matter on Earth were converted into binary information that was instantly cloned into dozens of 4D copies on the billions of hard-drive hybrids that were now scattered across the surface of the earth like a giant farm of plastic and metal mushrooms.

All the skin, bones, tendons, muscles, blood and lymph, veins and arteries, the nervous tissue, gland tissue, all the visceral matter, hair, teeth, nails, eyes, noses, mouths, ears, thoughts, regrets, memories, dreams, our own little personal history full of joy and disappointments, our bodies of gore and glory, were now packed tightly into a few cubic centimetres of computer memory.

In the second stage, the matrix of the info-matter was infected with the virus of The Salvation, propagated through all the multitudes of universes and hyperspaces, which had started beating together, like a single heart, all whispering His Name.

The prophecy had been fulfilled. We had all become immortal. *Death will be no more, and there will be no more crying, lamenting, pain, because those first things are over.* The girl next to me wiped her tears with the back of her hand. I took her hand, and she smiled at me happily. Then I saw on her right shoulder a tattoo: a picture of herself, eyes closed, a blue revolver held to her head. Above the tattoo, in Gothic script: *Ahora Y Siempre*. At the very last moment, the air filled with the transient smell of lavender. Then the Son of the Machine blew toward us and we all scattered into the Universe, bit by byte, like dandelion fluff.

```
      010                    0110
     00100                  001110
      101                    0110
       1                       0
       0                       1
0001100000110000111111111001111001
      00                      101
      00                      101
      00                      101
    0010100                 1101011
   10    01               11  1  11
   10    01               10     11
   10    01               10     11
   10    01               10     11
   10    01               10     11
  1000   0001            0111    1110
```